THE

BASS

SAXOPHONE

TWO NOVELLAS

THE
BASS
SAXOPHONE

by **JOSEF ŠKVORECKÝ**

Translated from the Czech by
KÁČA POLÁČKOVÁ-HENLEY

 Alfred A. Knopf · **New York** · **1979**

"Red Music" first appeared in the United States in *Persea II.*

Grateful acknowledgment is made to the following for
permission to reprint previously published material:

Atrium Verlag, Zurich, for permission to reprint four lines
from *Lyrische Hausapotheke* by Dr. Erich Kästner.
AG, Zurich, Switzerland 1946.

Farrar, Straus & Giroux, Inc. for permission to reprint
an excerpt from *I Wonder as I Wander* by Langston Hughes,
Copyright © 1956 by Langston Hughes. Used by permission
of the publisher.

New Directions Publishing Corp. for permission to use an excerpt from "Lament for the Months" from Tennessee Williams's *In the Winter of Cities.* Copyright 1944 by Tennessee
Williams. Reprinted by permission of New Directions.

Emöke was originally published in Czechoslovakia by
Československy spisovatel, Praha, under the title *Legenda
Emöke.* Copyright © 1963 by Josef Škvorecký. *The Bass
Saxophone* appeared in a volume entitled *Babylónsky příběh*
published by Svobodné Slovo· Melantrich, Václavské náměstí,
Praha, under the title *Bassaxofon.* Copyright © 1967 by
Josef Škvorecký.

English Translation first published in Canada by
Anson-Cartwright Editions 1977 Toronto

Library of Congress Cataloging in Publication Data
Škvorecký, Josef. The bass saxophone.
Translation of the author's Bassaxofon and Legenda Emöke.
I. Polačková-Henley, Káča.   II. Škvorecký,
Josef. Legenda Emöke. 1979.   III.   Title.
PZ4.S619734Bas   1979 [PG5038.S527] 891.8'6'35   78–7270
ISBN 0–394–50267–1

Manufactured in the United States of America
First American Edition

"But jazz is decadent bourgeois music,"
I was told, for that is what the Soviet Press
had hammered into Russian heads.

"It's my music," I said, "and I wouldn't
give up jazz for a world revolution."

LANGSTON HUGHES

CONTENTS

ACKNOWLEDGMENTS

With thanks to Marc Mercer

for his translation of the Emöke blues,

and to Eric Young and Mark Sarner

for their helpful criticism and support.

PREFACE

RED MUSIC

In the days when everything in life was fresh — because we were sixteen, seventeen — I used to blow tenor sax. Very poorly. Our band was called Red Music, which in fact was a misnomer, since the name had no political connotations: there was a band in Prague that called itself Blue Music and we, living in the Nazi Protectorate of Bohemia and Moravia, had no idea that in jazz blue is not a color, so we called ours Red. But if the name itself had no political connotations, our sweet, wild music did; for jazz was a sharp thorn in the sides of the power-hungry men, from Hitler to Brezhnev, who successively ruled in my native land.

What sort of political connotations? Leftist? Rightist? Racialist? Classist, Nationalist? The vocabulary of ideologists and mountebanks doesn't have a word for it. At the outset, shortly before the Second World War when my generation experienced its musical revelation, jazz didn't convey even a note of protest. (Whatever shortcomings the liberal republic of T. G. Masaryk may have had, it was a veritable paradise of cultural tolerance.) And no matter what LeRoi Jones says to the contrary, the essence of this music, this "way of making music," is not simply protest. Its essence is something far more elemental: an *élan vital,* a forceful vitality, an explosive creative energy as breathtaking as that of any true art, that may be felt even in the saddest of blues. Its effect is cathartic.

But of course, when the lives of individuals and communities are controlled by powers that themselves remain uncontrolled — slavers, czars, führers, first secretaries, marshals, generals and generalissimos, ideologists of dictatorships at either end of the spectrum — then creative energy becomes a protest. The consumptive clerk of a workingman's insurance company (whose heart had reportedly been moved by the plight of his employer's beleaguered clients) undergoes a sudden metamorphosis to become a threat to closely guarded socialism. Why? Because the visions in his *Castle,* his *Trial,* his *Amerika* are made up of too little paper and too much real life, albeit in the guise of nonrealist literature. That is the way it is. How else explain the fact that so many titles on Senator Joe McCarthy's index of books to be removed from the shelves of U.S. Information Service Libraries abroad are identical to many on the index issued in Prague by the Communist Party early in the seventies? Totalitarian ideologists don't like real life (other people's) because it cannot be totally controlled; they loathe art, the product of a yearning for life, because that, too, evades control — if controlled and legislated, it perishes. But before it perishes — or when it finds refuge in some kind of *samizdat* underground — art, willy-nilly, becomes protest. Popular mass art, like jazz, becomes mass protest. That's why the ideological guns and sometimes even the police guns of all dictatorships are aimed at the men with the horns.

Red Music used to play (badly, but with the enthusiasm of sixteen-year-olds) during the reign of the most Aryan Aryan of them all and his cultural handyman, Dr. Goebbels. It was Goebbels who declared, "Now, I shall speak quite openly on the question of whether German Radio should broadcast so-called jazz music. If by jazz we mean music that is based on rhythm and entirely ignores or even shows contempt for melody, music in which rhythm is indicated primarily by the ugly sounds of whining instruments so insulting to the soul, why then we can only reply to the question entirely in the negative."* Which was one reason we whined and wailed, rasped and roared, using all kinds of wawa and hat mutes, some of them manufactured by ourselves. But even then, protest was one of the

* *Týden rozhlasu*, Prague, March 7, 1942.

lesser reasons. Primarily, we loved that music that we called jazz, and that in fact was swing, the half-white progeny of Chicago and New Orleans, what our nonblowing contemporaries danced to in mountain villages, out of reach of the *Schutzpolizei*, the uniformed Security Service. For even dancing was forbidden then in the Third Reich, which was in mourning for the dead at the Battle of Stalingrad.

The revelation we experienced was one of those that can only come in one's youth, before the soul has acquired a shell from being touched by too many sensations. In my mind I can still hear, very clearly, the sound of the saxes on that old, terribly scratchy Brunswick seventy-eight spinning on a wind-up phonograph, with the almost illegible label: *"I've Got a Guy," Chick Webb and His Orchestra with Vocal Chorus.* Wildly sweet, soaring, swinging saxophones, the lazy and unknown voice of the unknown vocalist who left us spellbound even though we had no way of knowing that this was the great, then seventeen-year-old Ella Fitzgerald. But the message of her voice, the call of the saxes, the short wailing and weeping saxophone solo between the two vocal choruses, they all came across. Nothing could ever silence them in our hearts.

And despite Hitler and Goebbels the sweet poison of the Judeonegroid music (that was the Nazi epithet for jazz) not only endured, it prevailed — even, for a short time, in the very heart of hell, the ghetto at Terezín. The Ghetto Swingers . . . there is a photograph of them, an amateur snapshot, taken behind the walls of the Nazi-established ghetto during the brief week that they were permitted to perform — for the benefit of the Swedish Red Cross officials who were visiting that Potemkin village of Nazism. They are all there, all but one of them already condemned to die, in white shirts and black ties, the slide of the trombone pointing diagonally up to the sky, pretending or maybe really experiencing the joy of rhythm, of music, perhaps a fragment of hopeless escapism.*

There was even a swing band in the notorious Buchenwald, made up for the most part of Czech and French prisoners. And since those were not only cruel but also absurd times, people were put behind barbed wire because of the very music that was played inside. In a concentration camp near Wiener Neustadt sat Vicherek, a guitar player who had sung Louis Armstrong's scat chorus in "Tiger Rag" and thus, according to the Nazi judge, "defiled musical culture."† Elsewhere in Germany several

---

* One of the Ghetto Swingers, Eric Vogel, survived; now a music critic in the U.S.A., he wrote about them in an article in *Down Beat*.

† L. Dorůžka, I. Poledňák, *Československý jazz*, Prague 1967, p. 71.

swingmen met a similar fate and one local Gauleiter issued an extraordinary (really extraordinary? in this world of ours?) set of regulations which were binding for all dance orchestras. I read them, gnashing my teeth, in Czech translation in the film weekly *Filmový kurýr*, and fifteen years later I paraphrased them — faithfully, I am sure, since they had engraved themselves deeply on my mind — in a short story entitled "I Won't Take Back One Word":

1. Pieces in foxtrot rhythm (so-called swing) are not to exceed 20 percent of the repertoires of light orchestras and dance bands;

2. in this so-called jazz type repertoire, preference is to be given to compositions in a major key and to lyrics expressing joy in life rather than Jewishly gloomy lyrics;

3. as to tempo, preference is also to be given to brisk compositions over slow ones (so-called blues); however, the pace must not exceed a certain degree of allegro, commensurate with the Aryan sense of discipline and moderation. On no account will Negroid excesses in tempo (so-called hot jazz) or in solo performances (so-called breaks) be tolerated;

4. so-called jazz compositions may contain at most 10 percent syncopation; the remainder

must consist of a natural legato movement de-
void of the hysterical rhythmic reverses char-
acteristic of the music of the barbarian races
and conducive to dark instincts alien to the
German people (so-called riffs);

5. strictly prohibited is the use of instruments
alien to the German spirit (so-called cowbells,
flexatone, brushes, etc.) as well as all mutes
which turn the noble sound of wind and brass
instruments into a Jewish-Freemasonic yowl
(so-called wa-wa, hat, etc.);

6. also prohibited are so-called drum breaks
longer than half a bar in four-quarter beat
(except in stylized military marches);

7. the double bass must be played solely with the
bow in so-called jazz compositions;

8. plucking of the strings is prohibited, since it
is damaging to the instrument and detrimental
to Aryan musicality; if a so-called pizzicato
effect is absolutely desirable for the character
of the composition, strict care must be taken
lest the string be allowed to patter on the sor-
dine, which is henceforth forbidden;

9. musicians are likewise forbidden to make vocal improvisations (so-called scat);

10. all light orchestras and dance bands are ad-
vised to restrict the use of saxophones of all
keys and to substitute for them the violoncello,
the viola or possibly a suitable folk instrument.

When this unseemly Decalogue appeared in that story of mine* in Czechoslovakia's first jazz almanac (it was in 1958), the censors of an entirely different dictatorship confiscated the entire edition. The workers in the print shop salvaged only a few copies, one of which got into the hands of Miloš Forman, then a young graduate of the Film Academy in search of material for his first film. After several years of writing and arguing with the censors, we finally got official approval for our script, whereupon it was personally banned by the man who was at that time the power in the country, President Antonín Novotný. That was the end of our film. Why? Because the decrees of the old Gauleiter were once again in force, this time in the land of the victorious proletariat.

But back in the days of the swastika it was not just that one isolated German in the swing band at Buchenwald, not just the few imprisoned pure-Aryan swingmen — many far more reliable members of the master race were tainted with the sweet poison. How vividly I recall them, in their blue-gray Nazi uniforms, recently arrived from Holland with Jack Bulterman's arrangement of "Liza Likes Nobody," in exchange for copies of which we gave

---

* Editor's note: "I Won't Take Back One Word," published finally in 1966 as *Eine kleine Jazzmusik*. The detailed story of the intrigue surrounding *Eine kleine Jazzmusik* may be found in Josef Škvorecký's *All the Bright Young Men and Women*, Peter Martin Associates, Toronto, 1971.

them the sheet music for "Deep Purple" and the next day they were off to Athens, where there were other saxophones swinging, underlined with Kansas riffs. I can see those German soldiers now, sitting in a dim corner of the Port Arthur Tavern, listening hungrily to the glowing sounds of Miloslav Zachoval's Big Band, which was the other, far better swing band in my native town of Náchod. Vainly did I dream of becoming one of Zachoval's swingers. Alas, I was found lacking in skill, and doomed to play with the abominable Red Music.

How naïve we were, how full of love and reverence. Because Dr. Goebbels had decided that the whining Judeonegroid music invented by American capitalists was not to be played in the territory of the Third Reich, we had a ball inventing aliases for legendary tunes so that they might be heard in the territory of the Third Reich after all. We played a fast piece — one of those forbidden "brisk compositions" — called "The Wild Bull," indistinguishable to the naked ear from "Tiger Rag"; we played a slow tune, "Abendlied" or "Evening Song," and fortunately the Nazi censors had never heard the black voice singing "When the deep purple falls over sleepy garden walls . . ." And the height of our effrontery, "The Song of Řešetová Lhota," in fact "St. Louis Blues," rang out one misty day in 1943 in eastern Bohemia, sung in Czech by a country girl, the lyrics composed so that they might elaborate on our new title for W. C. Handy's theme song: "Řešetová Lhota . . . is where I go . . . I'm on my way . . . to see my Aryan folk. . . ." In fact, we were fortunate that the local Nazis had never seen Chaplin's *The Great Dictator,* never heard the bullies sing about the "Ary-ary-ary-ary-aryans." Neither had we, of course — "The Song of Řešetová Lhota" was simply an indigenous response to Nazism.*

It was, like most of our songs, ostensibly the composition of a certain Mr. Jiří Patočka. You would search for his name in vain in the lists of popular composers of the time since he too was a figment of our imagination. That mythical gentleman's large repertoire also included a tune indistinguishable from "The Casa Loma Stomp." In our ignorance we hadn't the faintest idea that there was a castle of that name in distant Toronto. We believed that Casa Loma was an American band leader, one of the splendid group that included Jimmy Lunceford, Chick Webb, Andy Kirk, the Duke of Ellington (Ellington had been placed among the nobility by a Czech translator who encountered his name in an American novel and decided that this must be a member of the impoverished British aristocracy, eking out a living

---

* Řešetová Lhota in the title of the Czech version of "St. Louis Blues" is the equivalent of, for example, Hicktown, Backwaterville, or Hillbillyburgh.

as a bandleader at the Cotton Club), Count Basie, Louis Armstrong, Tommy Dorsey, Benny Goodman, Glenn Miller — you name them, we knew them all. And yet we knew nothing. The hours we spent racking our brains over song titles we couldn't understand . . . "Struttin' with Some Barbecue" — the definition of the word "barbecue" in our pocket Webster didn't help at all. What on earth could it mean: "walking pompously with a piece of animal carcass roasted whole"? We knew nothing — but we knew the music. It came to us on the waves of Radio Stockholm mostly, since that was the only station that played jazz and that the Nazis didn't jam. Swedish style: four saxes, a trumpet plus rhythm — perhaps the first distinct jazz style we knew, except for big band swing. Curiously there was one film, also of Swedish provenance, that amongst all the Nazi war-propaganda films, the *Pandur Trencks* and *Ohm Kruegers,* escaped the eyes of the watchmen over the purity of Aryan culture. In translation it was entitled *The Whole School Is Dancing.* The original title appealed to us more, even though we understood no Swedish: *Swing it, magistern!* In the territory of the Third Reich, that was the movie of the war. We all fell in love with the swinging, singing Swedish girl called Alice Babs Nielsson, another reassuring indication that though we lacked knowledge we at least had an ear for jazz: much,

much later she recorded with Ellington. But that
film — I must have seen it at least ten times. I
spent one entire Sunday in the movie theater,
through the matinee, through the late afternoon
show and the evening show, inconsolably sad that
there was no midnight mass of *Swing it, magistern!*

"Swing it, magistern, swing it!" became one of
the standard pieces played at public concerts in
obscure little towns in eastern Bohemia, much to
the joy of fans of swing. But of course, enemies
of jazz and swing were also to be found amongst
our Czech contemporaries. The milder ones were
the jazz conservatives to whom swing was an out-
landish modern distortion. They would just boo
loudly at our concerts. The radicals, the polka
buffs, did more than that. They threw apple cores
at us, rotten eggs, all kinds of filth, and the legendary concerts in the legendary hick towns often
ended in a brawl between the polka buffs and the
fans of swing. Then the band would have to flee
by the back door to save their precious instruments,
irreplaceable in wartime, from the wrath of the
protectors of the one and only true Czech music:
the polka — played, horror of horrors, on an accordion.

The polka buffs never dared throw eggs at our
Ella, though. Yes, we even had our own Goddess,
our Queen of Swing, Girl Born of Rhythm, Slender
Girl with Rhythm at her Heels, our own Ella. She

was white, of course, and her name was Inka Zemánková. She distinguished herself by singing
Czech lyrics with an American accent, complete
with the nasal twang so alien to the Czech language.
My God, how we adored this buggering-up of our
lovely language for we felt that all languages were
lifeless if not buggered up a little. Inka's theme
song was something entitled "I Like to Sing Hot,"
not one of Jiří Patočka's ostensible compositions
but a genuine Czech effort. The lyrics describe a
swinging girl strolling down Broadway with "Harlem syncopating in the distance." It contained
several bars of scat, and concluded with the singer's
assertion, "I like to sing Hot!" This final word,
sung in English, alerted the Nazi censors, and on
their instructions Inka had to replace it with the
equally monosyllabic expression "z not," — a
charmingly absurd revision, for although it rhymes
with "hot," the expression means exactly the opposite of singing hot music: it means singing from
sheet music, from the notes.

Far from Harlem, from Chicago, from New
Orleans, uninformed and naïve, we served the
sacrament that verily knows no frontiers. A nucleus
existed in Prague that published an underground
magazine entitled *O.K.* (not an abbreviation of "Ol
Korekt" but of *Okružní Korespondence*, i.e., Cir-
culating Correspondence). Pounded out on a type-
writer with about twenty almost illegible carbon

copies, this underground publication (really underground, its very possession punishable by a stint in a concentration camp) was our sole source of reliable information. It was distributed through the Protectorate by lovely *krystýnky* on bicycles, the bobby-soxers of those perished times. I can see them in their longish skirts, dancing and "dipping" in the taverns of remote villages, with one fan always standing guard at the door, on the lookout for the German police. When a *Schupo* appeared over the horizon, a signal was given, and all the *krystýnky* and their boyfriends, the "dippers," would scurry to sit down to glasses of green soda-pop, listening piously to the Viennese waltz that the band had smoothly swung into. When the danger had passed, everyone jumped up, the Kansas riffs exploded, and it was swing time once again.

Then the Great War ended. In the same movie theater where I had once sat through three consecutive showings of *Swing it, magistern!* I sat through three screenings of a lousy print of *Sun Valley Serenade*, with Russian subtitles. I was impervious to the Hollywood plot, but hypnotized by Glenn Miller. The print had found its way to our town with the Red Army, the film badly mangled by frequent screenings at the battlefront, the damaged soundtrack adding Goebbelsian horrors to "In the

Mood" and "Chattanooga Choo-choo." Nonetheless, I had the splendid feeling that, finally, the beautiful age of jazz had arrived.

My mistake. It took only a lean three years before it was back underground again. New little Goebbelses started working diligently in fields that had been cleared by the old demon. They had their own little Soviet bibles, primarily the fascistoid *Music of Spiritual Poverty* by a V. Gorodinsky and I. Nestyev's *Dollar Cacophony*. Their vocabulary was not very different from that of the Little Doctor, except that they were, if possible, even prouder of their ignorance. They characterized jazz and jazz-inspired serious music by a rich assortment of derogatory adjectives: "perverted," "decadent," "base," "lying," "degenerate," etc. They compared the music to "the moaning in the throat of a camel" and "the hiccuping of a drunk," and although it was "the music of cannibals," it was at the same time invented by the capitalists "to deafen the ears of the Marshallized world by means of epileptic, loudmouthed compositions."* Unfortunately, these Orwellian masters soon found their disciples among Czechs, who in turn — after the fashion of disciples — went even further than their preceptors, declaring wildly that jazz was aimed at "annihilating the people's own music in their souls." Finally the

---

* *Hudební rozhledy* III, No. 17, 1950–51, p. 23.

aggressive theoreticians even organized a concert of "model" jazz pieces composed to order for the Party's cultural division. It was an incredible nightmare. Bandleader Karel Vlach, the greatest among Czech pioneers of swing, sat in the front row, going from crimson to ashen and from ashen to crimson again, probably saying a prayer in his soul to Stan Kenton. Beside him sat an unholy trinity of Soviet advisors on jazz (led by, of all men, Aram Khachaturian, colleague of Prokofiev and Shostakovitch), gloomy, silent, and next to them a senile choirmaster using a hearing aid. And yet not even the emasculated musical monster presented to them satisfied the Soviet advisors. They criticized its "instrumental makeup" and described it as "the music of a vanishing class." Finally, the old choirmaster rose, and we heard him add the final chord: "Now, take the trumpet. Such an optimistic-sounding instrument! And what do those jazz people do? They stuff something down its throat and right away it sounds despicable, whining, like a jungle cry!"

After that Vlach was unable to refrain from a few heretical remarks: if they didn't give him something better than Stan Kenton, said he, he would keep on playing Stan Kenton. Which is perhaps what he did, in the traveling circus to which he was shortly thereafter relegated along with his entire band. The Party also proclaimed the creation of an "official" model jazz band, and in the Youth Musical Ensembles the most avid ideologists even tried to replace the hybrid-sounding (therefore supposedly bourgeois) saxophones with the nonhybrid (therefore more proletarian) violoncello — but it takes at least five years to learn to play the cello passably, while a talented youth can master the saxophone in a month, and what he wants to do is play, play, play. But ideological thinking follows paths free from the taint of reality. In place of Kenton, they pushed Paul Robeson at us, and how we hated that black apostle who sang, of his own free will, at open-air concerts in Prague at a time when they were raising the Socialist leader Milada Horáková to the gallows, the only woman ever to be executed for political reasons in Czechoslovakia by Czechs, and at a time when great Czech poets (some ten years later to be "rehabilitated" without exception) were pining away in jails. Well, maybe it was wrong to hold it against Paul Robeson. No doubt he was acting in good faith, convinced that he was fighting for a good cause. But they kept holding him up to us as an exemplary "progressive jazzman," and we hated him. May God rest his — one hopes — innocent soul.

But in the early fifties, although the bishops of Stalinist obscurantism damned the "music of the cannibals," they had one problem. Its name was

Dixieland. A type of the cannibal-music with roots so patently folkloristic and often (the blues) so downright proletarian that even the most Orwellian falsifier of facts would be hard put to deny them. Initiates had already encountered isolated recordings of Dixieland during the war, and after it ended a group of youths heard the Graeme Bell Dixieland Band performing at a Youth Festival in Prague. They created the first Czechoslovak Dixieland Band, and soon there was a proliferation of Louisiana sounding names: Czechoslovak Washboard Beaters, Prague City Stompers, Memphis Dixie, and dozens of others. Uncle Tom music was really the only form of jazz suffered at the depressing congregations called youth entertainments, where urban girls in pseudo-national costumes got up and sang bombastic odes to Stalin in the style of rural yodeling.

An apostle of Dixieland, Emanuel Uggé, took the Czechoslovak Dixieland on the road. Once again, obscure little towns in the northeast of Bohemia resounded with loud syncopations, wound around with the boring, hyperscholarly commentaries of this devoted *Doctor Angelicus* of Dixieland who, for the ears of the informers attending the concert, succeeded in interpreting the most obscene tune from the lowest speakeasy in Chicago as an expression of the Suffering Soul of the Black People, waiting only for Stalin and his camps, where re-education was carried out directly for the other world. But it turned out that going on the road with Dixieland was a double-edged move. On the one hand, it kept the knowledge of jazz alive, but on the other hand what the more enlightened and therefore less brazenly orthodox supervisors in Prague had passed off as a "form of Negro folklore," the true-believing provincial small-fry recognized for what it was: an effort to "smuggle Western decadence into the minds of our workers. . . . Such orchestras conceal their vile intentions in music that has no educational merit," says a letter from the Town Council of Hranice to the Management of the Hranice Cement Workers. "Eighty percent of what the ensemble played was Westernist, cosmopolite music which had an eccentric effect, going so far as to cause one of the soldiers to come up on the stage and do a tap dance."* Horrors! A soldier in the Czech Red Army, tap-dancing to some Nick La Rocca tune! Years later I recalled this Harlemized soldier when I read in an article by Vasily Aksionov (author of the epochal *A Ticket to the Stars* — but who in the West has heard of him? Who knows that the liberating effect of this novel, written in Moscow slang, had perhaps a more profound influence on contemporary Russian prose than *Doctor Zhivago?*)

---

* L. Dorůžka, I. Poledňák, *op. cit.*, p. 102.

about a big band that existed somewhere in Siberia during Stalin's last days, and played "St. Louis Blues," "When the Saints," "Riverside Blues." . . . Another chapter in the legends of apostles who were often martyrs.

Even Inka, our idolized Queen of Swing, became one. After the war she had put aside her career in order to study singing professionally. Five years later, she decided it was time to make her comeback. The concert agency booked her for a Sunday matinee at the Lucerna Hall in Prague. She sang one song just before the intermission and was to sing another one after. It was an old swing tune, and while Inka's sense of rhythm had remained, her vocal range had doubled. She was rewarded by thunderous applause, gave them an encore, and this time sang one whole chorus in scat. The applause was endless. "When I stumbled offstage," she told me years later, "I thought to myself — there, I've made it again! But there was a guy there, in one of those blue shirts, you know, I think they called them the Young Guard,* all scowling and furious, and he yelled at me, 'That's it! Out! I can assure you you'll never sing another

---

* The blue shirt was the uniform of the Czechoslovak Union of Youth. Inka's ignorance of the name of this all-pervasive Party satellite organization was just an indication of her political naïveté. One interesting note: the fellow in question, one of those whose god has failed, now lives in exile in Switzerland.

note in public.' And in fact, that's what happened, they didn't even let me sing my second number after the intermission." At that moment I couldn't help thinking about Vicherek and his scat chorus in "Tiger Rag" during the Nazi occupation.

However, with the passage of years political events threatened the unlimited rule of the provincial small-fry (and the blue-shirted Communist Youth storm trooper) and also the validity of their musicological opinions. We began to consider how we might get permission for the Czechoslovak Dixieland Band (now metamorphosed into the Prague Dixieland Band) to perform in public again — and found unexpected and unintended help from the U.S. An American bass player named Herbert Ward had asked for political asylum in Czechoslovakia, "delivering another serious blow to American imperialism" the Party Press announced. It also said that Ward used to play with Armstrong. We immediately looked him up in his hotel in Prague and talked him into playing a role of which he was totally unaware and which is referred to in Stalinist slang as "shielding off." In fact, we used him ruthlessly. We quickly put together a jazz revue entitled *Really the Blues* (title stolen from Mezz Mezzrow), printed Herb's super-anti-American statement in the program, provided the Prague Dixieland to accompany Herb's home-made blues about how it feels to be followed by American secret police agents (a particularly piquant blues in a police state where everybody knew the feeling only too well), dressed his sexy dancer-wife Jacqueline in original sack dresses borrowed from a Prague matron who had lived it up in Paris in the twenties, then settled down to enjoy her dancing of the eccentric, decadent Charleston. Since Herb's terribly shouted blues had anti-American lyrics and because Jackie's skin was not entirely white the authorities didn't dare protest, and left us alone with our towering success. The show finally folded as a result of difficulties of a more American nature. Herb and Jacqueline wanted more money. The producer, bound by state norms, was unable to give them more, and *Really the Blues* died a premature death. Later on, Herb and Jacqueline went the way of many American exiles: back home to the States, the land where the words "you can't go home again" generally seem not to apply. Apply they do, though, for other countries, the ones that send their own writers into exile, to prison, or to their death.

Really the Blues was the end of a beginning. Jazz had grown to resemble the Mississippi, with countless rivulets fanning out from its delta. The Party found other targets: Elvis Presley, little rock'n'roll groups with guitars electrified and amplified on home workbenches, with a new crop of names recalling faraway places — Hell's Devils,

Backside Slappers, Rocking Horses — new outcries from the underground. By the end of the fifties, a group of young people had been arrested, and some of them sentenced to prison for playing tapes of "decadent American music" and devoting themselves to the "eccentric dancing" of rock'n'roll. (Again the spirit of Vicherek was present at their trial.) And because the mass of young people had turned to follow other stars, jazz proper, whether mainstream or experimental, was no longer considered dangerous, and so the sixties were a time of government-sponsored International Jazz Festivals. The stage at Lucerna Hall in Prague echoed with the sounds of Don Cherry, the Modern Jazz Quartet, Ted Curson. . . . We applauded them, although, for the most part, this was no longer the music we had known and loved. We were the old faithfuls. The broad appeal of the saxes was gone, either this was esoteric music or we had simply grown old. . . . Jazz is not just music. It is the love of youth which stays firmly anchored in one's soul, forever unalterable, while real live music changes, forever the calling of Lunceford's saxophones. . . .

That was when I wrote "The Bass Saxophone," and I was writing about fidelity, about the sole real art there is, about what one must be true to, come hell or high water; what must be done to the point of collapse, even if it be a very minor art, the object of condescending sneers. To me literature is forever blowing a horn, singing about youth when youth is irretrievably gone, singing about your homeland when in the schizophrenia of the times you find yourself in a land that lies over the ocean, a land — no matter how hospitable or friendly — where your heart is not, because you landed on these shores too late.

For the steel chariots of the Soviets swung low, and I left. Jazz still leads a precarious existence in the heart of European political insanity, although the battlefield has shifted elsewhere. But it is the same old familiar story: a specter is again haunting Eastern Europe, the specter of rock, and all the reactionary powers have entered into a holy alliance to exorcise it — Brezhnev and Husák, Suslov and Honecker, East German obscurantists and Czech police-spies. Lovely new words have emerged from the underground, like the *krystýnky* and the "dippers" of the Nazi era: now there are *Manichky*, "little Marys" for longhaired boys, *undrooshy*, from the Czechified pronunciation of the word "underground," for rock fans of both sexes. Anonymous people hold underground Woodstocks in the same old obscure hick towns, gatherings often ruthlessly broken up by police, followed by the arrest

of participants, their interrogation, their harass-
ment, all the joys of living in a police state.

And so the legend continues . . . and the chain
of names. The Ghetto Swingers, the nameless bands
of Buchenwald, the big band in Stalin's Siberia, the
anonymous jazz messengers in Nazi uniforms criss-
crossing Europe with their sheet music, the Lenin-
grad Seven — nameless aficionados who in the
Moscow of the sixties translated, from the Czech
translation of original American material, into
Russian *samizdat* the theoretical anthology *The
Face of Jazz* — and other buffs and bands, even
more obscure, blowing away for all I know even in
Mao's China. To their names new ones must be
added, the Plastic People of the Universe, and
DG307, two underground groups of rock musicians
and avant-garde poets whose members have just
been condemned (at the time I am writing this) to
prison in Prague for "arousing disturbance and
nuisance in an organized manner." That loathsome
vocabulary of hell, the vocabulary of Goebbels, the
vocabulary of murderers. . . .

My story is drawing to a close. *"Das Spiel ist
ganz und gar verloren. Und dennoch wird es weiter-
gehen. . . ."* The game is totally lost. And yet it
will go on. The old music is dying, although it has
so many offspring, vigorous and vital, that will,
naturally, be hated. Still, for me, Duke is gone,

Satchmo is gone, Count Basie has just barely survived a heart attack, Little Jimmy Rushing has gone
the way of all flesh. . . .

> . . . *anybody asks you*
> *who it was sang this song,*
> *tell them it was* . . .
> *he's been here, and's gone.*

Such is the epitaph of the little Five-by-Five. Such
is the epitaph I would wish for my books.

J.Š.

Toronto, 1977

EMÖKE

TO SÁRA

who knows it all

all too well

Give them, O mother of moths and mother
*   of men,*
Strength to enter the heavy world again,
For delicate were the moths and badly wanted
Here in a world by mammoth figures haunted!

TENNESSEE WILLIAMS

A story happens and fades and no one tells it. And yet somewhere, someone lives on, afternoons are hot and idle and Christmases come, that person dies and there is a new slab with a name on it in the graveyard. Two or three people, a husband, a brother, a mother, still bear the light, the legend, in their heads for a few more years and then they die too. For the children it remains only like an old film, the out-of-focus aura of a vague face. The grandchildren know nothing. And other people forget. Neither a name nor a memory nor even an empty space is left. Nothing.

But a certain building, a recreation center — once a hotel maybe, a rural inn or a boarding house — still hides the story of two people and their folly, and perhaps the shades of its characters may still be glimpsed in the social hall or in the Ping-Pong room, like the materialized images of werewolves in deserted old houses, trapped in the dead thoughts of human beings, unable to leave for a hundred, five hundred, a thousand years, perhaps forever.

The room's ceiling slanted downward. It was a garret, the window high off the floor — you couldn't see out unless you pushed the table over to the wall and climbed up on it. And the very first night there (it was a hot night, August, the susurrus of ash and linden under the window like the distant rush of diluvial seas, the window open to let in the night's sounds and fragrances of grass and grasshoppers and crickets and cicadas and linden blossoms and cigarettes and from the nearby town the music of a Gypsy band playing Glenn Miller's old "In the Mood," but in an undulating Gypsy rhythm, and then "Dinah," and then "St. Louis Blues," but they were Gypsies — two fiddles, a bass, a dulcimer — and the beat wasn't boogie but rather the weaving pulse of the Gypsy, the leader embellishing on the blue tones in a swaying Gypsy rhythm), the schoolteacher began to talk about women. He talked in the dark, in bed, in a hoarse voice trying to get me to tell him how it was with me and women. What I told him was that I was getting married before Christmas, that I was marrying a widow called Irene, but all the while I was

thinking about Margit and about her husband who
had let it be known that he would beat me senseless
if ever I showed my face in the district of Libeň
again, and about the carnival in Libeň and about
Margit with her nose red from crying, red like the
nose of the painted clay dwarf down in the desolate,
funereal garden behind the hotel, the inn, that recreation center or whatever it was. Then he began to
talk about women himself; words full of salacious
images, vulgar, raunchy, came pouring from his
craw, from his rabbit brain, evoking in me a profound depression. It was as if the hand of Death
were reaching out to me from the barren life of that
country schoolteacher, fifty years old with a wife
and three children, teaching at a five-grade school
and shooting off his mouth here about women, about
sex with young teachers whose work placement card
had forced them to leave their mothers and move,
with just a couple of worn suitcases, far away to
God knows where in the Sudeten mountains, to a
village near the border, where there wasn't even a
movie house, just a tavern, just a few lumberjacks,
a few Gypsies, a few locals transplanted here by all
sorts of plans and desires and dreams and bad con-
sciences, and just a deserted manse and the chair-
man of the local National Committee — before the
revolution a day-laborer on the estate of the lords
of Schwarzenberg, in his blood the congenital defiance of forefathers who had sweated over soil they

never owned, he had been driven here afterward
by that very defiance, that hunger for land; now he
had his land, and he sweated over it like all his
sinewy and unshaven forefathers had done except
that now the soil was his — and then the teacher, the
only one in the whole village who knew how to play
the violin and who could drop words like Karel
Čapek, Bedřich Smetana, Antonín Dvořák, words
that embodied the magic of virginal patriotic ideals
and the spirit of the Teachers College where young
women were prepared for that most beautiful of
professions; and when he first arrived there at the
age of forty he already had a wife and (at that
time) two children, but he told the young teacher
he loved her, in heavy calligraphy he wrote love
letters and poems that seemed almost familiar to
her (he had an old handbook of love letters and
love poems by anonymous poets that he would adapt
to his particular needs), and of a morning she
would find a bunch of primroses on her desk, or a
sprig of edelweiss or a bachelor's button or a spray
of lily of the valley, and she used to listen to him,
go to meet him beyond the village in the shrubbery,
in the underbrush of the pine woods where the wind
of late summer blew over the bald hills and the
town stood below, cold with the church spire pointing up to heaven, dingy, yellowish, half-deserted
under the steel-gray moss of autumn clouds, and
then she said Yes and took him to her room and

now he was telling me about it ". . . she said the light was too bright, that she was embarrassed, but all she had was a lightbulb hanging on a cord from the ceiling, no lampshade, nothing, so I pulled the panties off her, blue jersey flimsies they were, and hung 'em over the lightbulb, and right away it was like it used to be in the streetcars during the war, in the blackouts, and then I did it to her. . . ." He was a man entirely in the sway of death, and I swayed under the bleakness of that life of his, more desolate than the life of a mouse or a sparrow, or the caged armadillo at the zoo that just stamps its feet on the steel floor and snorts greedily and rhythmically and then eats and then copulates and snorts and stamps and runs around and sleeps because it's an armadillo, a comical beast that lives an optimum life according to armadillo law; but he was a human being, until recently principal of a five-grade school and member of the local National Committee although he had now been downgraded to the two-room school on the frontier ("The inspector had it in for me, a Party man, you know, he was jealous because he couldn't make time with a young teacher like I could"), heir to that ancient tradition of schoolmasters who in days of old brought books and music and beauty and philosophy into mountain cottages and to little villages like that village, husband to a wife who had to stay behind alone and was receiving a bonus for having to maintain a separate household, father by this time to three children, and here he was, living according to the laws of white mice and armadillos.

The girl (not the young teacher, but the one that sat next to us that first evening in the dining room listening to the social director, who called himself our Cultural Guide, unfolding an extensive and substantial program of organized activity for our group) was built like a dancer, slender as a street lantern, with boyish hips and delicate sloping shoulders, and breasts like the breasts of stylized statues, that did not disturb the slender young symmetry of the jersey-clad body. And almond eyes, gazelle's eyes, dark as the charred core of a charcoal pile, and hair like a Gypsy's but brushed to the flat sheen of black marble. We had walked beside her the whole day on an excursion to Mariatal, a place of pilgrimage to which believers used to come from all over the Austro-Hungarian Empire and perhaps from all over Europe (now it was a deserted and desolate forest valley) and I felt timid by her side, and most conversation topics seemed trivial and irrelevant. It was impossible to talk with her about the usual things, to have the sort of conversation where the words mean nothing or no more than the crowing of a rooster or the hooting of an owl calling to his mate from the crown of a pine tree. It seemed to me that with her one could only talk about ideas. She wasn't the kind of girl you approach at a dance and say, May I have this dance, miss? and then something about how good the band is and that's a pretty dress she has on and what's her phone number, and then you call that number and she either comes or she doesn't, and if she comes you go dancing again, and then you don't have to say much of anything any more, it's just a matter of whether you have an apartment or a studio or even just a furnished room with a close-mouthed landlady, or if you have none of these, at least enough money for two rooms in a hotel. No, this girl was profound, a philosophy of life rested somewhere in the depth of her soul, and you had to talk about that philosophy — it was the only way you could get to her, there was no other way. Of course, the schoolteacher didn't see that and he persisted with his noises, his vulgar expressions, crude conversational lines from common dance halls, the smart remarks of village Don Juans and small-town wolves; he trotted out the old tricks and clichés that call for an exact phrase, a precise response from a girl — like the Latin dialogue between priest and altar boy — in the eternal sexual ritual of establishing acquaintance, but she didn't come back with those petrified responses, she was silent and just said Yes (she was Hungarian, she spoke a strange combination of Slovak and Hungarian and some Gypsy or Carpathian dialect) or No, and the schoolteacher soon exhausted his stock of tricks

and ploys and fell silent, plucked a blade of grass
from the roadside, stuck it in his mouth and walked
along chewing on it, defeated and mute with the
grass sticking straight out of his mouth. Just then
a huge dragonfly flew across the path and I asked
the girl whether she knew that there were once
dragonflies with a wingspan of two and a half feet.
She voiced surprise and wonder that such a thing
was possible, and I began to talk about the Meso-
zoic Age and the Cenozoic Age and about Darwin,
about the world's evolving, the blind and inevitable
course of nature where the strong devour the weak
and animals are born to seek food, procreate, and
die, how there's no significance to it, significance
being a human term and nature a bare causal nexus,
not a colorful, meaningful, mystical teleology. And
that was when she told me I was mistaken, that nature does have significance, and life too. What significance? I asked, and she said, God. "All right,
knock it off now," said the schoolteacher. "Say, miss,
don't you feel like a beer? It's hotter than hell today." But she shook her head and I said, You believe
in God? I do, she replied, and I said, There is no God.
It would be nice if there were, but there isn't. You
haven't come that far yet, she explained. You're
still a physical person, you're still imperfect. But
some day you'll find Him. I, I said, am an atheist.
I used to be an atheist too, she replied, until my
eyes were opened. I discovered Truth. How did it

happen? I asked sarcastically, because she was slender like a dancer, and I knew dancers do go to church a lot and kneel and make the sign of the cross but they don't believe in God, they don't really think about God, they retain God as a superstition, the way they get someone to spit on them before they go on stage, before they don their professional smile and run out into the glow of the spotlights with their tiny little steps. When I got married, she said, and the schoolteacher, who had been walking alongside in silence chewing on a fresh piece of grass, awoke from his dumb stupor and said, "You're married?" No, she replied. I'm a widow. But when I was married, I learned to believe. Your husband was religious? I asked. She shook her head. No, she said, he was very physical, he had nothing in him of spiritual man. "That makes you a young widow, eh?" said the teacher. "And would you like to get married again?" No, said Emöke (her name was Emöke, she was Hungarian, her father, a postal clerk, had made a career for himself in Slovakia when part of that country was annexed by Hungary before the war: he had been sent there as postmaster and had begun to live like a lord, with a piano, a salon, and a daughter at the lyceum who received private French lessons), I'll never marry again. Why are you so determined? I asked. Because I have discovered that there can be more elevated aims in life, she replied. For

instance, you said that the eternal changing of
shapes has no significance, that it's all just cause
and effect. That is the way it appears to you. But
I see a significance in it that you don't see yet. What
sort of significance? I asked. It is all aimed toward
God, she said. Toward becoming one with Him.
That is the significance, the meaning of all life.

Between believers and nonbelievers there is no
communication, there is a wall, a steel barrier
against which understanding shatters. I did what I
could to explain to her that significance and meaning, and the sense of design which people attribute
to the blind activity of nature, are merely human
concepts, that that was what I'd been trying to say,
that meaning is an anthropomorphic idea born of
the awareness that every human activity has
"meaning" of one sort or another: we cook so that
we may eat, go on vacation to relax, brush our
teeth so they won't decay — and then we carry over
this idea of purpose to nature where we feel that
it is lacking; but she just smiled at all my logic
and my rationale and my helpless fury (it wasn't an
angry fury, just a desperate fury at the fact that
I couldn't convince her of such obvious truths, that
there was something in her, an ability or an inabil-
ity, something beyond logic, that proudly resisted
reason) and she replied to it all with a mild, calm,
almost sublime smile and the words, You are simply
a physical person. You are still imperfect. So I

asked her whether she didn't feel hatred for me or contempt that I was an atheist, and she shook her head and said, I pity you. Why? Because you may have to live many lives before you become perfect. And before you find the truth. Many lives? I asked. Yes, replied Emöke. Because you must become a spiritual person before you see the truth. "You mean you believe in reincarnation, miss?" asked the schoolteacher. It doesn't matter what it is called, she said. You needn't even use the name God. Words don't matter. But you must know the Truth.

We entered the forest valley of Mariatal where the little white pilgrims' church stood deserted, the broad lane of deserted booths leading up to it, smelling of rotting wood. The plank-top counters where gingerbread hearts were once stacked in piles beside holy pictures and mirrors with pictures of the shrine, and the decaying beams from which black, white, and pink rosaries had hung alongside silver and gold madonnas on chains, miniature fonts for holy water with pictures of the Mother of God, tin crucifixes, wooden ones with tin Christs, carved ones and plain ones, blessings for cottage parlor walls, pictures of the Virgin of Mariatal, pictures of saints and wax figurines, and beside them a booth where a fellow in a white apron with a fez on his head would chop slabs of Turkish honey-nougat into sticky sweet flakes, and a little farther on, a stand with chenille scarves, cotton stockings and glass jewelry, and a stand for sausages and another booth with holy pictures; and peasants in black suits and black hats wiping their sweaty faces with red bandannas, their black, laced boots dusty from the long trek, and little old ladies in white Sunday kerchiefs, and tired children, and weary couples who had come here to say a prayer for the success of their young marriage or the conception that was long in coming, and old people for a happy final hour, the sound of organ music coming from the church, and the sound of singing, the path curving up the hillside through the woods, bordered by little white chapels with wooden altars displaying hand-painted scenes from the lives of the saints, now long faded and peeling, aged by many rains and the hard heat of summer; and the Cultural Guide, his hairy, spindly legs protruding from his shorts, climbed up on to the steps of one of the chapel pavilions (that first evening he would expound on his plans for our recreation, but the second night he got drunk and the third day he was sleeping it off and the last evening at the farewell party he drank himself speechless and rolled under the platform where the musicians tipped the spit out of their saxophones onto him) and began to lecture us about the pilgrimages that used to come here — it was immediately apparent that he was totally ignorant not only of the Catholic Church, its dogma, liturgy, tradition, and catechism, and of Biblical history, but of everything in general; he made a joke about sterile women and impotent men coming here to Mariatal to pray for the restoration of their juices, and then he waxed serious and launched into an exposé of religion, a splendid mishmash of the most desperate vulgarization of Engels, science pre-masticated for narrow minds — presented to us to salve his own conscience for the twelve-hundred-crown salary he was paid each month — not science popularized for the unschooled though spontane-ously intelligent mind of the workingman, but rather cheap half-truths and quarter-truths for parasitical leeches who don't give a damn about truth, not science but pseudo-science, cut-rate science, a derision and an insult to science, not truth but stupidity, a lack of sensitivity, a lack of feeling, a thick-skinned denseness impervious to the arrows of that tragically desperate poetry of a desperate dream that is to come to pass only in the hereafter of the utopian world of future wisdom (in the absence of drunken bums who feel a revulsion for manual labor and make a living by spouting ill-learned phrases memorized from tour-guides to ancient cas-tles), the poetry of sunny pilgrimages with the voice of the organ underscored by the wail of paper whistles, and the smell of evergreens and pine needles mingling with the sweet smell of incense, and little altar boys in red and green collars, their lace-up boots poking out from under their robes,

fervently bobbing the smoking censers, and the loveliness of the forest and its light and shadow and
the call of the cuckoos parting to the stride of the
priest dressed in gold who lifts the shining mon-
strance with the glowing white circle (the most
perfect plane figure of the ancient Greeks) in its
glittering center and holds it suspended over the
bowed heads in kerchiefs and the gray hair of old
farmers so that it seems to float on wisps of smoke
from the burning incense, flooded by the glow of
sun and forest light like a symbol of that eternal
human longing and hope which will be realized
here and on this earth, but which is unattainable,
unthinkable without this poetic folk faith in the
goodness which rules the world in the long run,
faith in love, faith in justice; a faith, hope, and
love that had never entered the mind of this
drunken, vulgar, dense Cultural Guide.

In our room that night the schoolteacher said to
me, "Seems to me you're not very good at handling
women. That's no way to go after a broad. Religion
and dinosaurs? At that rate you'll never get her to
bed within the week, you can bet your life on it."

Later, Emöke told me about him. The schoolteacher had got up early and prowled around under
her window, baring his yellow teeth at her, yelling
his wisecracks up to her whenever she appeared at

the window to take down the white socks she washed each evening and hung out below on a taut string to dry. The schoolteacher rutted under the window while she gave him a cool and polite good morning, and he made his proposition, "Don't you want to flush out your lungs, miss, the woods are full of ozone of a morning!" and she shook her head and told him No and he went off by himself and then all day he circled around her, his eyes glowing in his self-indulgent face, his brain chewing the cud of the few ideas at his command, not ideas, conversational stereotypes, and from time to time he would come up to her, pull one out and lay it on her, and having failed go off again, his eyes still glowing, observing her hungrily from a distance, circling around her like a ruffled rooster around an inaccessible hen from another barnyard. She told me her story, her legend. It was like the confidences that prostitutes are said to impart to their clients of girlhoods in aristocratic households, the fall and the poverty and the sorrowful selling of one's body. She told me how they had stayed in Slovakia after the war, about her Hungarian father, a small-time official and a fascist, who had been a supporter of the Nazis and was destroyed after the war, no pension, no livelihood, too old and sick to take a job digging ditches or cutting down trees, and her mother, broken and loathing physical work, and herself, sixteen, in her sixth year at the Hungarian lyceum

that the Slovaks closed down, when along came this
man, the owner of a farm, and vineyards, he was
rich, forty-five, with a hotel in Bratislava, and she
had given in to him to save her family from misery
or death by starvation or old age in the poorhouse,
he was overbearing, mean, dense, he didn't believe
in anything, God, democracy, human decency,
nothing, just himself, and he wanted a son to inherit
his farm and hotel and vineyards, but he wasn't
prejudiced, he didn't mind that she was Hungarian.
She bore him a daughter and that day he stormed
out and drank himself dumb, he didn't speak to
her for a week and then he began to beat her when
he was drunk; that was when a hearty, hard-drink-
ing bunch began to meet at the farm, cars would
drive up from Bratislava, from Košice, from Tur-
čanský Svatý Martin, there were meetings in his
study and he became a member of a right-wing
party, but she didn't pay any attention and when
he came to her at night, his breath stinking like a
wine cellar, he would force her to do what for him
might still have been pleasure but for her was
suffering and shame; as she got to know this man
with the bull neck and the heavy breath, she also
discovered her Truth: she had met another man, a
gardener who had tuberculosis and who later died,
and he lent her books about the path to God, the
developing of one's spiritual strength, the spiritual
universe and life beyond the grave, and she came to

believe that everything here is nothing but one immense process of purging oneself of the stain of evil, and evil is matter and man must purge himself of matter, of the body, of desire, his goal must be the spirit, but not even that, for the spirit is just another stage, a higher stage than the physical one, and the ultimate aim is to reach God, to become one with Him, to dissolve one's own self in the infinite horizon of bliss that radiates mystical divine Love and Goodness.

Soon after, her husband was killed. After the Communist coup in February 1948 they nationalized his hotel, then his farm, and then they arrested him; he escaped, but they shot him as he tried to swim the Danube to Austria. She got a job in an office and learned bookkeeping, becoming a good bookkeeper; she went to live in Košice with her little girl (her parents were both dead) and she wanted to raise her little girl in the truth that she herself had discovered.

She lent me some of those books. They were bound collections of various parapsychological and theosophical journals; I found an article on the powers of amulets and the effectiveness of copper circlets which, when worn on the naked skin at the perihelion of Mars, will protect the wearer from rheumatism and bleeding, and I asked her whether it didn't seem strange to her that people who place so much emphasis on the spirit should be so con-

cerned with the body since three quarters of those
theosophical formulas concerned protection against
disease, and whether she believed it all. She replied
that at each stage of one's existence one must obey
the laws that come from God, and the laws of physical existence call for attention to one's physical
well-being. And as for the formulas, she asked how
I could admit I had never tried them yet claim I
doubted their effectiveness. So you too, she said,
are imperfect and reject the truth, everyone rejects
the truth, but in the end everyone will discover it,
because God is Mercy. And with those words, a
curious look came into her eyes, a flash of anxiety,
as if she were afraid I wanted to rob her of something, of the certainty she possessed and without
which she couldn't survive, couldn't bear the burden of her widowhood, the burden of death and of
a sad, destroyed life; it was the expression of an
ensnared little woodland animal, begging you with
its eyes not to torture it and let it go, to release it
from your power.

The schoolteacher asked me how I was making
out. I knew that I had her, like the little animal in
the woods, strangely in my power, the way men
sometimes capture women without deserving to and
without really trying, by the simple inscrutable
effect of attraction and submission, but I didn't
understand it the way I had at other times, or as
I did with the ordinary, erotic, and uncomplicated

Margit; this time it was as if the invisible nerves that linked us were nourishing some sort of drama, some possible fulfillment that might wipe out the desperate and vicious illusion which had made of that slender body and that lovely face and those delicate dancer's breasts and that creative force a chimerical existence imprisoned in a vicious circle.

The schoolteacher frowned, growled, and rolled over in bed so hard that the springs creaked.

Two days before our week's vacation was due to end, it rained, and the vacationers played Ping-Pong or cards or sat around in the dining room, chatting about things, trying for a while to find someone to play the piano; the Cultural Guide awoke from the previous day's drunkenness and tried to bring the group together with some game he called French Mail, but the only ones he could interest were an old married couple: he, paunchy, with baggy knee-breeches, a former owner of a haberdashery, now manager of a state-owned clothing store in Pardubice, and she, fat, benign, at fifty still emitting the naïve peeps of surprise that she used to emit at eighteen on the merry-go-round: she always revived at lunchtime, not out of gluttony but because food was the only thing she understood, otherwise she moved through life in a mist, guided by the light of secure conventions, maternal admonitions, dancing lessons, nice boys carefully picked by her parents, courtship, marriage, two or three births, and Sunday mass (but if anyone were to ask her about even the most basic theological terms, she wouldn't know what to say, she simply went to mass, sang the hymns in the hymnal, genuflected, beat her breast, made the sign of the cross with the tips of her fingers moistened in holy water, and had requiem masses served in memory of her late mother); her kitchen too was an island of security where she became an artist, a virtuoso with absolute pitch for tastes and odors, like a violinist can tell a quarter tone and even an eighth, not rationally but intuitively, with a sense that others don't have and can't have, something that isn't the result of the five or seven years of apprenticeship in a mother's kitchen but a gift of grace, a piece of immortality given to a person in addition to the simple ordinary skills and the sleepy brain with its few stunted thoughts, and a heart submerged in lard, capable of no dishonesty or evil, capable only of an animal love for its young, its spouse, its family, for people, for life, and of resignation to death — the last of those beacons of security that border the path from the first moment of awakening in the mists of life. Then the Cultural Guide also found an old seamstress for the game, an old maid, a worker laureate of the state enterprise called Gentlemen's Linens, who was spending her first vacation away from her home in Prague's working-class

Žižkov district, and who had spent the entire week so far sitting around, standing around, walking around, not knowing what to do, with nothing to talk about because she didn't know anyone there and in all her life hadn't known anything but men's shirts, had never known a man and love, had lived frozen between the prose of shirts and the primitive poetry of the dreams of old maids. He also got hold of a pimply young hot-shot who had tried in vain the first three days to gain the affections of a pig-tailed Slovak girl, who in turn had given preference to a black-haired technician, a former gunner in the R.A.F., who had a wife and child at home but had learned the art in which the schoolteacher would never be more than a rank amateur and had taken it to the very pinnacle that that limited art could ever reach, and the hot-shot had got riled, retreating to the stubborn solitude of the recreation hall along with his striped socks and his black silk shirt, and now, sulky and defiant, he had been half talked into playing the game of French Mail. And finally the Cultural Guide had rooted out an uncertain, silent man who may have been a foreman in a factory or something but who never said a word to anyone, and with these people — people dominated by both the feeling of being obliged to enjoy themselves for a whole week, for the duration of this cheap if not entirely free vacation, and a feeling of helplessness as to how to go about it since they had all fallen victim to the fallacy that on vacation you can enjoy yourself in a manner different from the one to which you are accustomed, people who knew nothing but work, and for whom work was as essential as air and food, and who had been suddenly called upon to live the life of men and women from a bygone era, men and women unfamiliar with work: wives of wealthy businessmen, of officers, physicians, stockbrokers, sons of rich fathers, or tanned daughters of the sweet bourgeoisie for whom free time was all the time and amusement a vocation that they understood — and now, with these people burdened with the onus of vacationing, the Cultural Guide, with his hangover, and a cup of black coffee in his hand, began a collective game in order to maintain the impression of his productivity, the illusion of having honestly earned the twelve hundred crowns of his monthly pay.

The schoolteacher lolled around the Ping-Pong room, glaring across the green table and through the glass wall into the dark, wood-paneled corner where I was sitting on a bench with Emöke; then he and a bespectacled self-taught Ping-Pong player played a game, the schoolteacher executing pseudo-virtuoso drives and smashes, most of them ending up in the net, but when once in a while he pulled something off after all, he would stab his hungry gaze in Emöke's direction to see if she was looking, and, taking long shots with the elegance of a lifeguard, low and easy, with an expression of bored pity, he beat the pants off the bespectacled enthusiast who played for fun and not for effect but lacked all talent for the game and kept chasing balls under the pool tables into all corners of the room.

I sat with Emöke in the dim light of the wood-paneled corner, drinking a toddy — although Emöke had Chinese tea because one shouldn't drink alcohol, alcohol debases one to the lowest level of physical being, transforms one back to the animal that one once was — and she talked about medical treatment by Paracelsus's methods, about trees that take upon themselves the diseases of men, just a small cut on a fingertip, a drop of blood pressed into a cut in the bark of a tree, and a bond is formed, a fine thread of delicate and invisible matter by means of which the man remains forever joined to the tree, as he remains forever joined to everything that ever left his body, a fallen hair, a breath, a clipped fingernail, and the illness travels along that thread to the tree and the tree fights the illness and overcomes it or sometimes perishes and dries up, but the man regains his health and his strength and lives on. She told about possession by evil spirits, exorcism by means of holy water and prayers, about black magic and evil powers that serve a person if he has the courage to stand in the center of concentric circles inscribed with the secret names of the Supreme One and intone evil prayers from

the Satanic psalter, backward, and she told about
werewolves, vampires, haunted houses, and witches'
sabbaths and her spirit stumbled in those dangerous
worlds that you don't believe in and you laugh at,
but once you have heard of them there is always a
tiny drop of horror in you, terror and fear. She
forgot about me and I was silent, she talked on
and in the gray light of the rain her eyes shone
with a sort of feverish, unhealthy, unnatural enthusiasm, and I was silent and watched those eyes
and she noticed it and the feverish shine faded
and I shook off the strange evil enchantment of
that magic rainy moment too, made a sarcastic face
and said, You don't mean to say you want to devote
yourself to black magic? Why, it's the epitome of
Evil and you're striving to attain Goodness. And
she dropped her gaze and said, Not any more I
don't want to, but once I did. When? I asked. When
I couldn't stand it any more, she replied, when
I began to feel God didn't hear me, that He'd
turned against me. I wanted to ask the Evil One
for help, to — to help me get rid of him. And did
you? Did you make those concentric circles with
consecrated chalk? I asked. No, she said, God was
protecting me. I understand now that God is constantly testing man, and many people don't pass the
test. But why does He test them? I asked. To see if
man is worthy of the supreme grace of being de-
livered from everything physical, to see if he's

ready. But man never asked God to create him, I said. By what right does God test him? God has the right to do anything, she said, because God is Love. Is He supremely merciful? I asked. Yes, she said. Then why did He create man? Because He loved him, she said. And why did He create him, then? Why did He send him into this world full of suffering? To test him, to see if he is deserving of His grace, she explained. But isn't He torturing him that way? I asked. Why didn't He just leave him alone from the outset, if He loves him? Or, once he created him, why didn't He go ahead and create him perfect right off? Ready for eternal bliss? Why all the martyrdom of the pilgrimage from Matter to Spirit? Oh, you're still imperfect, she said. You reject the truth. I don't reject it, I said, but I want to have proof. And if not proof, then at least logic. Logic is also the work of God, she said. Then why doesn't God use logic Himself? He doesn't have to, she said. Some day you will understand. Some day everyone will understand and everyone will be saved. But don't talk about it any more, please, she said, and her eyes again had the look of a little animal in the woods, afraid of losing that one certainty of forest freedom; so I stopped talking about it and went over to the piano; Emöke came and leaned against the top and I began to play "Riverside Blues," which she liked, and then I sang "St. James Infirmary," and the schoolteacher came over

from the light and darkness of the Ping-Pong room
and stood behind Emöke and I was singing

> _I went down to Saint James Infirmary_
> _For to see my baby there_
> _Stretched out on a cold white table_
> _So sweet, so cold, so fair._

And the pentatonic melody born of that basic
human sorrow that can only end in a convulsive
lament — the sorrow of two people who are parting ways forever — slid into Emöke's heart and she
said, That's a beautiful song. What is it? It's a
Negro blues, I replied, and Emöke said, Yes, I've
heard that Negro people are very spiritual people,
I heard them sing some religious songs on a record,
one of the men at the office has records from
America. Ah, I said, blacks are lecherous rascals,
but they've got a great sense of music. It just seems
they're that way, she retorted. They are spiritual
people. And I played and sang some more, and
when I had finished, the schoolteacher said, "Come
on, beef it up a little and put some life into it, a
little jive so we can cut a rug, right, miss? This is
Dullsville, not a vacation!" So Emöke laughed and
told me to give up my place at the piano, and she
sat down and started to play with sure, naturally
harmonizing fingers, a slow but rhythmical song
that held the distant echo of a czardas, the pulse
of Hungarian music as unmistakable as the blue

notes in Negro blues, and she sang in an alto that
sounded like the level tone of a shepherd's flute,
that cannot be modulated, strengthened or weak-
ened, sure and straight and with a primitive beauty;
she sang in hard sweet Hungarian a song that was
neither sad nor happy but just desperate, her cheeks
flushed, and the song wasn't the chanting of a black
magician in concentric chalk circles but the call of
a shepherd on the steppe, ignorant of black sabbaths and black masses, living a natural life on
sheep's milk and cheese, sleeping in a wooden
shack, aware of a few superstitions but not associating them with God or the Devil, possessed once
in his life by such an insurmountable longing that
he goes off and sings this desperate, yearning, level,
unmodulated loud song in his unmodulated and
sweetly hard language and finds a mate and with
her conceives new shepherds and lives on, eating
cheese and whey by his evening fire, among the
smell of hides and charcoal in his shack. And then
I realized that that vulgar exhortation of the
adulterous schoolteacher had liberated her as if by
magic from the spectral world of things spiritual,
and that this song sprang from the immense sen-
suality in her, but I also knew it was just the
schoolteacher's words, not the schoolteacher himself, and suddenly I understood the catharsis toward which her drama was progressing, the fact
that the Evil One in her life was that middle-aged

owner of the hotel and the farm who had driven her
into the realm of dangerous shades, into the unreal
but frightening world of specters, so that she was
now seeking the Supreme Good, Love, spiritual,
nonphysical, divine; but that perhaps it would take
very little for all that warped symbolism of obscure
parapsychological magazines to be turned upside
down by a strange, incomprehensible, and yet
entirely comprehensible, flip of the soul, that the
Good and the Supreme could perfectly well be me,
that maybe that's what I already was, even if she
wouldn't admit it to herself, even if she didn't realize it yet, that maybe I was there already, in the
deep, unknown cellar rooms of her unconscious, or
at least getting there and at one stroke I might now
be able to change the story, the legend, I might
really become the Supreme One, the Creator, and
create something human of this beautiful shade
retreating slowly and surely into the mists of madness, that this mind was still capable, though not
for much longer, of turning from its blind alley
of uncertain imagery back onto the firm track of
things concrete — but not for much longer, soon
it would be lost in the twilight of the fogs that rise
from *terra firma* and, having lost all knowledge of
the law of gravity and all corollaries to that law,
swoop according to the law of fogs to the abyss of
senseless heights, possessing their own truth which
is not a lie because it is simply another world and

there is no communicating between this world and that one: a girl becomes a woman and a woman a crone, closing herself off in that world, encased in a network of wrinkles, her womb wasted and her soul slowly becoming a mournful litany of cracked old voices in the musty Gothic corridor from this world to the next, of which we know nothing and which perhaps is nothing.

"That was swell, miss!" said the schoolteacher when she stopped singing, and he started to applaud. "Now how about a czardas, what do you say?" She laughed and really began to play a czardas, emphasizing the beat with her entire body, her eyes glowing but not with the shiny feverish glow that they had had earlier in the wood-paneled corner. The schoolteacher stepped away from the piano and, yelping, performed a clumsy mock czardas (missing the beat entirely, and stamping his feet out of rhythm too) and as he wriggled ludicrously in front of the piano, Emöke began to sing again. Her singing attracted the group that had been playing French Mail and the athletic young girls and boys from the Ping-Pong room, and soon people began to enjoy themselves; I had to sit down at the piano again and play popular hits and some of the girls and boys and the schoolteacher and Emöke began to dance. Emöke had changed, like a bright butterfly's wing slipping out of a gray and mysterious cocoon, and this was she, not a legend

but the real Emöke, for the primitive and unconscious schoolteacher had primitively and uncon-
sciously found the right way to her buried heart
and her path to the future; but I knew that path and
future weren't destined to be his, because he wasn't
interested in her future, just in the brief present
of the week's vacation, in a lecherous thrill and a
lewd memory. I was the one who could follow that
path, but I'd gone too far along the path of my own
life to be able to throw myself into the future without stopping to think it over. The yellow piano keys
didn't want to return to their original position and
I pounded them to produce song after song, watching her, and all of a sudden, like the schoolteacher,
I began to desire that body, that slender, firm body,
those breasts that didn't disturb its symmetry. Yet
I realized it was all very, very complicated; I knew
that there's a prescription for such fevers (and the
schoolteacher would certainly prescribe it: sleep
with her — it'll solve everything) that is, by and
large, an effective prescription, but I also knew
that in Emöke's case this particular goal, the
physical act, would have to be preceded by something far finer and more complex than the schoolteacher's technique, and that it wasn't really a
matter of the act at all but of the commitment that it
represents, the act being merely a confirmation, a
confirmation of the union that people conclude
against life and against death, just the stigma of

the act of creation which, if I wanted to, I might
perhaps bring off; yet it wasn't that act of confirmation I yearned for (it would mean years and years
of my life and one knows that every enchantment
finally dissipates over the landscapes of the past
and all that remains is the present, everyday reality) but rather the body, the pleasant, unusual
vacation adventure, the womanly secret between
the girlish thighs; but that way, of course, if I didn't
take upon myself her whole life I would destroy
her, and so as Emöke danced with the schoolteacher,
I began to hate him with all my heart, this speci-
men who was not a man but a mere sum total of
screws, and as for her, I was mad at her, a primitive
masculine anger that she was dancing with him and
so wasn't what she had appeared to be until a while
ago; although I didn't agree with that world of hers
created of desperate wishes, I still preferred it to
the world of the schoolteacher.

So that when we met on the stairs on the way to
dinner, I asked her sarcastically why she showed so
much interest in the schoolteacher since he was
obviously a basely physical person; and she said
innocently, I know, he is a physical man, I felt
sorry for him. We must feel compassion for people
as unfortunate as he, and I asked her whether she
didn't feel any compassion for me, after all I was
physical too. Not entirely, she said. You at least
have an interest in things spiritual, he doesn't; sud-

denly she was again entirely different from the way she had been with the schoolteacher, that cloud from another world obscured her face, she sat down at the table with a monastic absence of mind, and the schoolteacher's hungry glances went unnoticed as did the stares of the hot-shot, who was beginning to weaken although he still clung to his role of offended lover of solitude.

The Cultural Guide announced that after dinner, at half past eight, there would be movies. Emöke went to her room and I went outside to the garden. It was damp, moldy, neglected. I sat down on a rotting bench wet through by the rain. Across from me stood the painted dwarf, his face rain-smudged, the tip of his nose knocked off, with a pipe between his teeth like the one my grandpa used to smoke; Grandpa used to have a dwarf like that in his garden too, with a pipe like that, and a white castle with lots of carved turrets and towers and real glass in the windows, and every spring he would paint the tin roof of the castle with red paint because at seventy-odd years the old man was still thrilled by the ideas that thrilled me when I was small, and thrilled me again at that moment when I remembered my grandfather's little castle: I believed that the castle was real — small maybe, but real — and that perhaps sometimes the half-inch steps were climbed by a royal procession of people two inches tall, like Lilliputians, that there were chambers

behind the real glass windows, and salons and ban-
quet halls just as realistic as the castle itself; and
then there was the fairy tale of Tom Thumb: I
dreamed of being Tom Thumb, riding around in a
car wound-up with a key, or sailing the bathtub in
a little boat that when you poured some chemical
into the stern sailed silently and regularly around
the miniature ocean of the enameled bathtub. I
stared at the ruddy, lecherous, beat-up ˙ıce of the
clay dwarf and in a way it was me, myself, thirty
years old, still single, mixed up in the affair with
Margit, a married woman, a guy who didn't believe
in anything any more or take anything very seri-
ously, who knew what the world was all about, life,
politics, fame and happiness and everything, who
was alone, not from incapacity but of necessity,
quite successful, with a good salary and reasonable
health, for whom life held no surprises and with
nothing left to learn that I didn't already know, at
an age when the first minor physical problems
begin to herald the passing of time, at an age when
people get married at the last moment so as still
to be able to have children and watch them grow
up only to find out equally fast exactly what life's
all about, and she, pretty and still young, with a
child, Hungarian and hence a fairly novel being,
relatively unfamiliar, but then again old enough
at twenty-eight, but with a child which I supposed
would mean an entirely different lifestyle, and a

foreigner, Hungarian, not too intelligent, slightly warped by that parapsychological madness, out to proselytize, but heaven knows how holy, the ideal object for a vacation adventure, nothing more than that, and yet with that terrible look of a little animal of the woods, with that immense self-destructive defense mechanism against the world, in a fog of mystical superstition. For her it was a matter of life and death, not a matter of a hot evening, a meadow soft enough to lie in comfortably, a few tried-and-tested words, a well-chosen moment when the desire of summer and the mood of the week's vacation blend to form a favorable constellation of discarded inhibitions and the will to risk and to surrender; it was in fact a matter of a lifetime of love and self-sacrifice, or of death in the mist of mysticism, in the lunacy of midnight circles that meet around round tables and summon the spirits of their visions to come to earth, circles of faded middle-aged people, misfits, psychopaths, in this twentieth century still believing in goblins and the power of frog hair over cancer, recopying Satanic psalters and speaking backward the terrible black prayers of men who had sold their souls to the Prince of Darkness — men who didn't die a natural death but were torn asunder by the Devil, their souls ripped out from the shreds of their bodies and the tatters of bone and flesh, broken ribs, gouged eyes, flayed skins, ripped out and carried

off to the eternal fire in the rotting guts of hell —
or praying piously and not eating meat and treating
ailments resulting from the constant immobility of
praying by placing copper circlets against their
bare skin and kissing pictures of saints, although
death should be desirable, since death is presumably the gateway to a more perfect plane of life,
closer to the Divine and eternal Bliss; that's what
it was a matter of, not a matter of a single night
but of all nights over many years, and not a matter
of nights at all but of days and mutual care, marital
love and good and evil until death do you part.
That's what it was a matter of with that girl, that
girl, that girl Emöke.

But later, sitting in the darkened auditorium
where the Cultural Guide was showing a film (after
several vain attempts to make the projector work,
and only after the silent fellow, who was perhaps a
factory foreman, had taken over, adjusting a screw
here and there, and the projector had rattled to a
start), a film that was precisely calculated for the
maximum possible nonentertainment (and yet the
people were entertained, because it was a movie and
the projector was rattling away behind their backs
and they were here to spend a week enjoying themselves), and as the room vanished in the smoky dusk
I took Emöke's hand, warm and soft, and because
tomorrow was the last day of our stay at the
recreation center and I had to do something — or at

any rate I succumbed to instinct or to that social obligation to seduce young women on vacation, single, married, or widowed — I asked her to come outside for a stroll. She acquiesced, I got up, she got up too and in the flickering of the projector I glimpsed the schoolteacher's gaze following her as she left the room by my side and went out into the night light of the August evening outside the building.

We walked through the night, along the white road between the fields, bordered by cherry trees and white milestones, the sweet smell of the blossoms and the countless voices of tiny creatures in the grass and the trees. I took Emöke's hand, she didn't object, I wanted to talk but I couldn't think of anything to talk about. There was nothing I might say, since my conscience kept me from opening the dam that held back my usual August evening rhetoric (irresistible to any lone woman on vacation providing the speaker is sufficiently young and not overly ugly) because I once again realized that it was a matter of life and death and that she was different, deeper, more inaccessible than other girls. I merely stopped and said Emöke, she stopped too, and said Yes? and then I took her in my arms or I moved as if to take her in my arms, but she slipped out of the incomplete embrace. I tried again, I put my arm around her slender, very firm waist and drew her toward me but she disengaged herself, turned and walked quickly away. I hurried after her, took her hand and again she didn't object, and I said Emöke, don't be angry. She shook her head and said, I'm not angry. But really, I insisted. Really, she said. It's just that I'm disappointed. Disappointed? I asked. That's right, replied Emöke. I'd begun to think you were different after all, but you aren't, you're just a prisoner of your body like all men. Don't be angry at me for it, Emöke, I said. I'm not angry, she answered, I know that men are usually like that. It's not your fault. You're still imperfect. I thought you were on the way, but you aren't, not yet. Not quite. And what about you, Emöke, I said, have you entirely given up everything physical already? Yes, replied Emöke. But you're so young, I said. Don't you want to marry again? She shook her head. Men are all the same, she said. I thought that I might find someone, some friend that I could live with, but just as a friend, you know, nothing physical, it disgusts me — no, I don't feel contempt for it, I know that physical people need it, there's nothing essentially bad about it, but it's derived from badness, from imperfection, from the body, from matter, and man progresses only by reaching toward the spirit. But now I've stopped believing that I'll ever be able to find a friend like that, so I'd rather be alone, with my little girl. She spoke, and her face was like milk, lovely in the

light of the stars and the moon and the August night.
I said, You won't find a friend like that. Not you.
Not unless it's someone like that consumptive gardener of yours, the one who used to lend you those
books because he wasn't capable of anything else —
Don't talk about him like that, she interrupted me,
don't be like that, please. But Emöke, really, I said,
don't you ever long for someone — I mean the way
girls do when they're as young as you and as pretty?
Do you honestly think you could find a friend who
wouldn't want that of you unless he were a poor
wretch, somehow disabled or crippled? Oh, but it's
not a matter of longing, Emöke replied. Everyone
has temptation, but one must overcome it. But why?
I said. What for? Longing needn't be exclusively
and solely physical. It can be an expression of love,
a yearning for oneness. Longing is at the very
source of existence, insofar as people are born of
love. You love your little daughter, don't you? And
don't you want to have any more children? You
could have them, I'm sure of that. Do you want to
give all that up, voluntarily? Emöke echoed, Give
it up? Everything is the will of God, she said. But
is God standing in your way? I asked. He gave you
so much, more than other women. You are young,
pretty, healthy, all men aren't like that first husband of yours, not all marriages are based on reasons like yours. There are men who love their wives
for more than just the physical side of marriage,

even though that too is a part of love — But it's not a part of true love, she exclaimed. True love is love of the soul. But how would you have children then? I asked. Or are you against children? Oh, no, she said, children are innocent and need love. But they're burdened with sin, and woman must suffer for that sin when she brings them into the world. That doesn't answer my question, I said, and besides, childbirth can be painless nowadays. But are you in favor of children being born at all? Wouldn't it be better just to give it up and not keep bringing new objects of sin or whatever into the world, new beings burdened by matter and physicality, because that's what most people are. Wouldn't it be better to let people die out? No, she retorted quickly. It's God's will that they live. In His infinite goodness, God wants all people to find salvation. And all of them will, one day. But what do you mean by "all"? I said. And when will they all find salvation? Wouldn't it be better to stop now, so that "all" would be "all those now living in the world"? No, no, no, she said. No, you don't understand. You're the one that doesn't understand, I replied. You don't understand your own self, you're full of inconsistencies. You haven't resolved a single thing for yourself, let alone thought about the logical flaws in your mystical system. Oh, what's logic! she said. Just a subject in school. No, it's everything, I answered. It's your appealing to me terribly, it's . . . my liking you a lot, and it's my . . . Don't say it, she whispered, ridding me of the need to pronounce that fatal set of words which in her case could not be taken back, which would carry its full meaning and not be just a vague promise to be broken or simply forgotten, because it was she, Emöke, that story, that legend, that poem, the past, the future.

We were standing in front of the illuminated entrance to the recreation center. She stared at the dark shadows of the trees against the night, and the expression in her eyes was no longer that of a forest animal but of a woman fighting off the primal damnation that is the root of her feelings of inferiority and the source of her life-giving force, and that can in one red flash blind thought and reason although it may end up in — well, in all that painful business and possibly the shame of being an unwed mother and the worry and the risk of getting fat and losing one's charms and one's life and everything. But that damnation overcomes a woman all the same, and she gives in the way she's always given in and always will give in, and it's of this damnation that a new human being is born. Good night, said Emöke, reaching out to shake my hand. Emöke, I said, think about it. Good night, she said and disappeared inside the hotel. I caught a glimpse of her slender legs on the stairway and then nothing. For a while I stood in front of the hotel and at last I went upstairs to my room.

The schoolteacher was lying in bed, his pants, shirt, shorts, socks, everything neatly hung up to air along the back of the chair and the foot of the bed. He was awake and he measured me with a mean look. "Well?" he said. I didn't answer him, I sat down on my bed and began to undress. The schoolteacher watched me with eyes like two dried-up black figs. "Well, I'll be damned," he said, "don't tell me you're going to sleep with a hard-on!" Aw, nuts, I said, turned off the light and lay down in bed. For a while there was silence. Then the schoolteacher said, "Seems to me that you're a dud. That you don't know how to handle women. Admit it!" Good night, I said. Beyond the window a rooster crowed, aroused from his night's sleep by a bad dream.

At the farewell party, I drank red wine and watched Emöke who was wearing a close-fitting summer dress with a white collar, her arms bare, dressed like any other attractive girl of her age. When the vacationers saw I was just sitting there drinking, they gradually grew bolder and asked her to dance (they hadn't dared before, because according to the rules of vacationers she and I comprised a

couple, and such a couple is a holy thing to these
one- or two-week collectives), and so Emöke was
constantly on the dance floor, one time with the
Cultural Guide, who was only half sober, once with
the hot-shot, who had given up sulking but hadn't
quite given up hope of living it up in what was left
of his vacation (specifically with one of the four or
five available girls in the group), once with the
paunchy manager of the clothing store, whose
pudgy wife observed her with the loving gaze of
matrons who would never think of being jealous
but who view young girls full of erotic charm as
sort of mystical sisters in the delusive destiny of
womankind, once with the leader of the jazz band,
who didn't dance or even put down his fiddle at any
other time during the evening, and with several
others, and I sat over my third glass of red wine,
for I was possessed by the strange indecisiveness
of a man who feels a sense of responsibility but is
still too much a man of his times not to have to
fight off indifference, frivolity, irresponsibility.
Emöke, the wine rose slowly to my head, Emöke on
the dance floor looked altogether different from
the five or six other girls on the dance floor; she
was the most graceful, youthful yet ripe, without
the imperfection of the seventeen-year-old face that
hasn't yet made up its mind whether to trade in
the loveliness of childhood for the shallow and
uninteresting beauty of adulthood or for the charm

of youth, the female charm of the age of courtship
and the first natural swell of fertility; she laughed
like they did, but hers was a deep alto laugh, and
she danced with the natural assurance of women
who know how to dance the way birds know how
to sing or bees to make a honeycomb, the body of a
dancer curving under the thin summer fabric of her
August dress; I looked at her and a wave of longing
and fondness for that desperate soul and, fortified
by the wine, a longing for the body and the breasts
swelled inside me until finally the wine which man
substitutes for woman's damnation (risking father-
hood, matrimony, his career, his whole life for the
deception of a brief moment) released me from all
bonds of reason and wisdom, and when I saw the
schoolteacher, his eyes lit up like those of a witch's
tom cat, emerge from somewhere in the dark re-
cesses of the hall and ask Emöke to dance and saw
him dance with her, pressing close to her body, half
a head shorter than she, a satyr with a satyr's
lecherous face but none of the mythic poetry, I
rose and broke onto the dance floor with a drunk-
ard's energetic gait and cut in and took Emöke
away from the schoolteacher. I hadn't seen her since
morning. I had spent the whole day in my room; the
schoolteacher had taken off but I had stayed in,
dozing and thinking about that girl, about all the
possibilities and my own insecurity and indecisiveness, but now I was with her, holding her around

the waist as I had last night only she wasn't pulling away from me this time, and I had the wine in my head and her eyes had lost their mystical mildness, the cloistered resignation of anaesthetized passions, and they were the eyes of a Hungarian girl, like stars over the *puszta,* and the inner rhythm that yesterday had made the keys of the old piano tremble now flowed through her slender legs and was transformed at her hips into the circular motion of a prelude to love.

The schoolteacher withdrew to a table with a small glass of white wine and wet his muzzle in that sourish liquid of village dances that infuses the stench of lust pantingly relieved with hot whispers and abandoned cries in fragrant orchards behind taverns or, when there isn't enough tail to go around, that simply goes the way of all liquids, flowing into the stinking tarred troughs of caustic smelling tavern toilets and from there to cesspools and from there into the earth which purifies the liquid and transforms it back into the crystal flow of the spring in the valley. He raised his heavy, mean, bloodshot eyes to the dance floor and followed me with the resentful stare of an outsider as I danced with the Hungarian girl; he knew I was young and single and an intellectual from Prague, one who had mastered that vague miscellany of information that evokes the impression of erudition he too was striving to evoke, and so at night, in pri-

vate, he would rail contemptuously against yokels
who get together at recreation centers, dumb-ass
shopgirls, mechanics who barely know how to sign
their names, and it never occurred to him that he
himself was capable of little more than signing his
own name in the heavy-handed calligraphy that was
a throwback to the days of the Austrian Empire,
that he didn't know much more than the four rudi-
mentary operations of arithmetic, the solution of a
quadratic equation and a brief review of Czech
history (memorized a long time ago by rote in the
so-called heroical-patriotic form of idealistic bourgeois stories about heroes and national spirit, and
now confused with a Marxism he had failed to
grasp), how to tell the male blossom from the
female on a few plants and how to classify the
common fauna of this planet into mammals, birds,
and invertebrates, but he didn't know a blessed
thing about Dollo's Law of Irreversibility or the
amazing evolution of turtles' shells, or the semi-
legendary archaeopteryx; he wouldn't believe you
if you told him that the brontosaurus had two nerve
centers in its spine and hence two brains, and if he
did happen to half believe you he'd transform it into
a crude joke. And yet he could stand in front of
runny-nosed children at their schooldesks, and with
an expression of extreme erudition lecture them
how, according to an English scholar named Darwin,
man is descended from the monkey, and over the

years he had grown used to feeling intellectually superior to the six- to eleven-year-old pupils around him, to the weary farmers who dropped in to the tavern on Saturdays for a drink, and village blacksmiths whose hands, accustomed to the weight of iron sledgehammers, were unable to sign their names in the box marked "parental signature" in their children's weekly reports without smearing the page with axle grease and without the uneven signature creeping beyond the narrow printed rectangle; he never considered that it is just as hard, if not harder, and just as worthy, if not worthier, and probably far more beautiful to be able to control the delicate mechanism of a precision lathe, to turn out silvery shining bolts and nuts, to observe the milky flow of oils and other fluids that flush and lubricate the cutters and drills, than it is to scratch out the natural expressions of childhood with red ink, molding them into uniform monstrosities of correct grammar and acceptable style, and to implant in children's souls such deep-rooted subconscious convictions as "i before e except after c," yet he did know that my erudition (even though it was only a glorified nonerudition, the kind of intellectual fraud committed by ninety-nine percent of all high school graduates with the exception of the one percent that become theoretical physicists, astronomers, paleontologists, paleographers, chemists and experimental pathologists) was greater, more impressive than his — as was my suit, made by a good Prague tailor, while his pudgy body, half a head shorter than Emöke's slouched in a Sunday suit of a style beyond style that had never even been in style, aggravated by a necktie in that eternal pattern of indeterminate slots and slashes; and so with his baleful, helpless eyes, eyes of the weak, the outcast, the handicapped, he followed me around the dance floor as I danced with Emöke.

For a long time, we didn't speak. I could feel her body, feverish with the inner warmth of young women, of the music, the stuffy room, the wine and the dance. We didn't speak to each other, and then the fiddler cut loose with a wailing, rapid Gypsy melody in a spasmodic rhythm, first a long drawn-out note, growing stronger, finally exploding into a brief syncopation, almost a dead end, to continue on another note, and Emöke began to sing in Hungarian, a hard, beautiful, primitive song of her nomadic ancestors, she was transformed once again into what she really was, a young girl concentrating all her energy in the essence of her female life, and we wheeled in some wild Hungarian dance, smudges of faces and figures and silver musical instruments spinning past as when a camera turns too quickly in a movie panorama.

I don't know for how long. For quite a while. Then toward midnight they began to play a tearful

and sentimental slow foxtrot, from his alto sax the
saxophone player drew the most heartrending sobs
that could ever be wrung from that most perfect
product of instrumental inbreeding, and Emöke
stopped singing and I began to talk, from somewhere out of my subconscious memory of the innu-
merable blues that have never failed to thrill me
came lines of verse, in triads, as they must come to
black guitarists high like I was high on wine, and
into Emöke's happy, lovely little ear I spoke line
upon line of the only blues I ever composed in all
my life, colored by that rural sax player who didn't
even know the secret of black syncopation and who
transformed the saxophone into a wailing instrument of cheap saccharine emotion made beautiful
by the primitive and eternal beauty of that convulsive, alcoholic moment, when the alcohol, man's
enemy but a greater friend, reveals to him the truth
about his own self, the truth about Emöke. First
time, first time, baby, last time, only time too. Short
time, short time, baby, first and last time too. We
wait such a hard long time for this time, what else
can we do? and Emöke stopped short, in the smoke-
screen of nicotine and spotlights above the tables I
could see her long charcoal lashes and I said, Like
a dying fire we wait to die, die in the flame. In a
living death we burn, burn in the cold rain. Fire
and ashes everything changes, still is the same. Now

is the time, I continued, for us to meet somehow, Just this time, lady, can we meet somehow? Listen, little darlin', to the sweet sound of now, and Emöke's lips, usually wilting, a convent rose of frosty asceticism, had broken into a smile, I said, Let me see you smile, laugh the whole night through. Smile for me now, smile the whole night through. Nobody for years, now he's here to save you, she looked at me, the smile on her lips, her eyes smiling the same smile, the saxophone wailing and moaning. Listen! See that flame glimmer in the night, see in infinite black, love's flickering light, Dark rain's over, love's season is in sight, and then Emöke laughed aloud and said, That's a nice poem! Who wrote it? But I shook my head and continued, This time, baby, this is my this time song. Coming at you from nowhere, it's here and then it's gone. Sing it for my little lady this time, this time song. Emöke threw her head back, the saxophone sobbed and groaned and the words flowed through me, on and on, from a strange inspiration never before and never since encountered, at that moment as beautiful as the Song of Solomon because this girl had never heard the like in her life, no one had ever called her the Rose of Sharon, no one had ever addressed her with that Pythagorean axiom of love, O thou fairest among women, because for all her short life she'd been no more than purchased prop-

erty, a hot-water bottle of flesh and blood and bones,
but now she was hearing it, a poem composed just
for her by a man, a poem flowing from a man's
heart, borne by the strange magic of this crazy age
of telecommunications from the heart and throat of
a half-stoned black shouter of the Memphis periphery to the vocal chords of a Prague intellectual in
this social hall in a recreation center in the Socialist
state of Czechoslovakia, but then she didn't know
anything about the picturesque genealogy of the
song, she perceived it only in the ideal manner of
perceiving poetry, because every poem is created
ad hoc, for some woman, and if it isn't, it's not a
poem, it's not worth reading or hearing since it
doesn't come from that unique, genuine and true
inspiration of all poetry; it seemed that she was
happy and she said in a whisper, May I believe
you? Do you really mean it? Yes, Emöke, I said,
and my soul or my heart or whatever it was, brought
forth more and more verses of those alcoholic,
triadic blues. I don't know, but at that moment I
entered into matrimony with her, at that moment
I gained a wisdom long forgotten by this age, an
awareness that marriage — the life of a man with
a woman — isn't, can't be, must not be that odd
jumble of passion and sentimentality, smut, and
gastronomic indulgence, complementary souls and
common interests, since it isn't a matter of under-

standing, equality of intellect, dovetailing personal-
ities and support and a balanced diet and the way to
a heart through a stomach, and it isn't that ludicrous
relationship canonized by Hollywood in the twenties and still adhered to in socialist-realist novels of
the fifties — a relationship valid at best for the
instinctive eroticism of adolescent infatuations or
for the fossils of middle-class Victorianism — and
that winds up in loathsome divorce proceedings
claiming the no less ludicrous relationship of con-
jugal incompatibility, but it is the relationship
between a male of the species and a female of the
species, the primal cave couple of two equal but
totally different individuals, one of whom has mastered the club and the other the fire, one of whom
brings home the game and the other kneads the
bread, together bringing their young into the world
according to the primal laws of the species, for the
unique beauty of perpetual regeneration, the joy of
sunlight on naked skin and of digestive juices and
the poetry of the blood and that finer joy of hearts
obedient to the law that man must again attain the
level of animals, but higher by one twist of the
spiral, and rid himself of the psychoneurotic dross
of conventional sentimentality that has been
sloughed off on the relationship of the human pair
by centuries of war and thievery and perverse
mysticism and male servitude and male dominance
(*Frauendienst ist Gottesdienst*).

But when I returned to the room (I had left for a moment, and in the corridor to the toilet — where I was singing blues without words, the way youth since the beginning of time has given voice to the joy of motion and rhythm by chanting unintelligible nonsense syllables in rapid succession — I got to talking with the leader of the jazz band who was making his way there too, fiddle in hand, and who recognized in me a brother in the international brotherhood of rhythmic, antiracist, antifascist syncopated music) I found Emöke dancing in the arms of the schoolteacher, who was telling her something with great urgency, and when he caught sight of me (I had stopped and was leaning against a column, watching them) the expression on his face changed unwittingly to that of someone caught doing something he shouldn't; when the piece ended he bowed to Emöke and went with untoward willingness over to his table and his white wine, fixing on me the black hate-filled eyes of a man avenging a defeat in the eternal struggle. I went over to Emöke and asked her to dance; she came but she was suddenly different, the membrane of monastic reserve once again obscuring her pupils. What is it, Emöke? What happened to you? I asked. Nothing, she said, but she was dancing lifelessly, passively submitting to my movements like an indifferent dance partner casually asked to dance in some dance hall into which a lonely young man has wan-

dered foolishly seeking diversion, seeking to fill a
lonely city afternoon with a casual dance with a
partner he doesn't know and who doesn't know him,
they dance a set of foxtrots together, in silence or
exchanging a few conventional phrases, neither ap-
peals to the other, they nod a bow and he leads her
to her table where there is a glass of soda-pop and
he says, Thank you, she nods again, they part and
forget each other's existence and he just sits there
looking at the half-empty dance floor of the half-
empty dance hall and he doesn't dance after that
and he goes home alone and lonely and goes to
sleep, devoured and torn by the indifferent isolation
of big cities. What happened to you? I insisted.
Something happened. There's something on your
mind, Emöke, tell me what it is. Then she turned to
me, and in her eyes, around her eyes, in the con-
figuration of the fine lines that comprise immediate
expression, there was painful surprise, the sorrowful self-deriding reproof of a woman who suddenly
realizes that she has once again done something she
swore she would never do again, and she said to me,
I'm sorry, but could you show me your identity
folder? For a millisecond I was startled, not painfully or offendedly, simply startled by that almost
official request, whereupon I felt a surge of fondness
for the simplicity, the straightforward, ordinary,
honorable way in which she took my offer of mar-

riage so matter-of-factly, the only right way, without the movie mysticism of fragile emotions, and instantly I knew it was the schoolteacher, that in his impotent rage the schoolteacher had convinced her I was a cheat, a married man taking a vacation from his marriage, and his dirty mind had transformed the fictional tale of my forthcoming marriage to a widow and the legend of Emöke into this ugly and yet logically credible tale, and immediately I felt a wave of tenderness toward Emöke, who had encountered that kind of man in her own marriage and was now terrified that I might be the same. I said, Emöke! Who gave you that idea? Of course I can show you my identity folder, and I reached into my inside breast pocket for that document that would confirm the truthfulness of my actions, my countenance, and she said, with an inexpressible sadness in her voice, Why are you lying to me? You don't have to show me anything. I know everything. But what? What? Emöke! There isn't anything to know! I said. Why do you deny it? she replied. I thought you were different, but you aren't. You aren't. You aren't. You're just the same as all the rest, she said. But Emöke! No, don't say anything, I know it all. Why don't you at least consider your fiancée's feelings, if you don't consider mine. Basically, I'm just a stranger, you've only known me a few days. But her feelings . . .

Emöke! That's nonsense! I exclaimed. It was that idiot schoolteacher who made you believe that. But he's lying! Can't you tell he's just a dirty old man? Don't call him names, she said. It was honorable of him to call my attention to it. But it's not true! Emöke! Don't lie, please. You showed him her photograph. But . . . (I had shown the schoolteacher a picture of Margit and her two-year-old son, Peter, I don't know why, maybe out of stupid male vanity). Then show me your identity folder if you say it isn't true, said Emöke, and that was when I remembered that the picture was in my identity folder; I had taken it out to show to the schoolteacher, and he had even told her that — Margit with the flirty bangs, the cleavage in the neckline of her summer dress, and with that sweet little blond two-year-old in the grass among the dandelions. I can't, I said weakly. But it isn't true. Don't lie, said Emöke. Please, don't lie at least. I'm not, I insisted, I'm not lying, but I can't show you the identity folder. Why not? I just can't. Because . . . Why? said Emöke with a penetrating look, and once again it was the little animal looking at me, but this time it was as if someone really had taken something away from it, an illusion of forest freedom, as if it were staring into the maw of a wild beast it hadn't known existed in its green and sunny world. Why can't you? she said urgently, in an excited voice that I hadn't heard her use before and the eyes of the little animal grew large as in the final, ultimate flash of comprehension beneath the yellowed fangs of the beast, and then the monastic pallor of her cheeks flushed an unnatural crimson and nervously, painfully, almost weeping, Emöke said quickly, Let me go, I have to leave. I'm taking the train at one o'clock in the morning. Goodbye! and she tore herself away and left the room swiftly, she disappeared while I stood there, she vanished.

I turned and saw the schoolteacher, squatting at the table, his face smoldering with wounded righteousness.

I was waiting for her at half-past midnight in front of the building, but she came out with her roommate, another Hungarian girl, in a group of about five Slovaks who were all taking the night train. It was obvious that she had asked the other girl not to leave her alone with me because she stayed close beside us the whole way. So I couldn't say anything to Emöke, I just asked her if I might write to her. Of course, she said, why not? And will you write to me? Why? she said. I lowered my voice so the other girl wouldn't hear and said, Because I love you, Emöke. Believe me. I don't

believe you, she replied. The other girl had stepped
aside a bit but she was still within hearing distance
so I had to keep my voice down. Believe me, I
repeated, I'll come to see you in Košice. May I?
Why not? she said. But will you speak to me? May
I visit you? Of course, she said. Then will you
believe me? She didn't reply. Will you believe me,
Emöke? She was silent a while longer. I don't know.
Maybe, she said after a pause, and by then we were
at the station, a little village station with the train
already waiting, and the uniformed stationmaster
standing beside it. The vacationers boarded, a
Slovak helped Emöke get her suitcase inside and
then she appeared like a black silhouette at the
carriage window. Emöke, I said, aiming my words
upward as if I were casting a spell on her, as if I
could draw from her an answer to the eternal and
monotonous question of my life, so empty with its
eternal variations on the love ritual, so sleazy, so
lacking in values, in honesty, in love, and yet so
bound up in the self-indulgent habit of illusory
freedom that I was unable to make up my mind.
Emöke, I said in the darkness, upward toward that
silhouette, that legend that was ending, and I heard
her Yes softly and from a great distance. Believe
me, please, I called weakly. Emöke! Yes, she said.
Goodbye, but it was no longer the call of a lonely
animal in the forest wilderness but the voice of

disappointed and skeptical wisdom, the voice of a woman who is being transformed into the image of time lost, and the engine started to rumble, the train moved, and a slender white arm waved to me out of the window, the arm of that girl, that dream, that madness, that truth, Emöke.

Overnight, the wine and the wisdom, the awareness or the vacation infatuation or whatever it was, evaporated and I awoke to the cold sober reality of Sunday morning, my imminent departure for Prague, my office, my colleagues, my pitiful affair with Margit and all the rest. The schoolteacher lay snoring on the other bed, his shorts, his shirt, everything carefully hung up to air again. I didn't say a thing. He disgusted me, for all the hygiene of his clean underwear, because the grime of his soul couldn't be aired out of his jockey shorts, his trousers or his shirt; he wasn't even human, just living breathing filth, an egotist, a lecher, an idiot, an enemy.

I didn't say a thing to him. He might have even denied it. It wouldn't have proved anything, and I wouldn't have achieved anything by an angry confrontation. I was silent. Yet in fact my time was coming, my moment of revenge — the only possible revenge, for it wounded him where he was most vulnerable, a revenge that he dug for himself like a grave, and into which he lowered himself helplessly.

But maybe it was Fate, the miller, the avenger, tyrant, friend, and lord who provided the means on that train rolling through the ripe August landscape, in pursuit of the curving track of the eternal sun, eternal within the bounds of human eternity, its shiny, reddening glory lighting up the faces in the compartment like kerosene lamps, transforming them into golden portraits: a childless couple of about thirty (a technical draftsman and his wife, who was a clerk at the State Statistical Agency), the taciturn factory foreman, the hot-shot, the manager of the clothing store, his wife, myself, and the schoolteacher. And the game began. It was the idea of the draftsman and his wife. They often played it; they had no children and they killed time by paying visits to other childless white-collar couples — every Thursday the wife played bridge and he played poker, and since they were members of a Hiking Club they would also go every Sunday in spring to a chalet in Skochovice where they played volleyball with the people from the neighboring chalets, and other games, when it grew dark, such as this familiar parlor game. It has a hundred names and like chess is played by everyone at some time or another; but this parlor game is more human than the empty and perverted feudal logic of chess which sucks so much energy from the human brain for the sake of the silly movement of bizarre figurines: here one person goes out of the room while the others decide on a certain object, person, animal, the Pope, Mars, the fruit preserves in one of the suitcases, or even the player himself (the one who went out of the room) and then they let him back in and he must eliminate everything, progressively and by using indirect questions requiring affirmative or negative replies, until by logic he arrives at the thing or the animal or person. The draftsman went out, and the clothing-store manager — as often happens with people who once in their lives stumble on something unusual, something which brightens their dull world of daily routine and polite clichés with a ray of wit, and which they'll then repeat at every possible opportunity — suggested that we choose him, the draftsman himself, as our subject, but the hot-shot, with little consideration for the man's feelings, declared that everybody does that and any fool would guess it right off; his own suggestion was that we take the Pope's left shoe as the subject. But the draftsman's wife decided that too few attributes of the object were known, such as the material, the shape, the color, and so forth. "No," she said. "We have to use something easier, so the ones who've never played the game will see how it's done." The schoolteacher and the wife of the clothing-store manager had declared they didn't know the game. The manager's wife was probably telling the truth, but not so the schoolteacher. I looked at him; he had the expression of a fat man forced to be It in a game of tag, totally at the mercy of slimmer players and destined to plod heavy and wheezing among human bodies tauntingly flitting past until someone takes pity on his helplessness and allows himself to be caught. He was lying. Obviously and visibly. He knew how to play the game. But he probably didn't like to play it. I knew why some people didn't like to play it. Not fat people, people who are slow in other ways. He was nervous. Then he noticed I was looking at him and suggested his suitcase, to keep up appearances.

"No," said the draftsman's wife, "that would be too easy. How about the Ping-Pong table in the recreation center?"

The draftsman was called in and he started with a query as to the concrete or abstract nature of the object.

"It's concrete," said his wife. A second later, the schoolteacher nodded. The wife of the clothing-store manager looked at the draftsman's wife with an uncertain questioning smile. Her eyes showed as much intelligence as those of the schoolteacher, but they lacked the nervousness. She displayed only wondering ignorance.

"Is it in Czechoslovakia?" asked the draftsman.

"It is," replied the schoolteacher, the manager's wife, and the hot-shot in unison.

"Is it in Prague?" asked the draftsman.

"No," replied the chorus, this time without the schoolteacher.

"Is it in K.?" asked the draftsman. (K. was the place we had just left, where the recreation center was.)

"No," replied the schoolteacher quickly.

"Oh, but it is!" the wife of the clothing-store manager corrected him with wondering reproof. "We said it's the —"

"Shhh, Mrs. M.!" exclaimed the draftsman's wife. "Yes, it's in K.," she told her husband.

"Then why did you say it wasn't?" the manager's wife asked, in the petulant voice of the naïve. "When it really is?"

"I just wanted to mix him up a bit," said the schoolteacher.

"But that's against the rules," said the draftsman's wife. "It wouldn't work that way."

"That's just what makes it exciting," he replied.

"Oh, no," said the draftsman's wife. "The point of the game is in having to answer truthfully, but in not being able to ask directly. So it's up to the person to show how smart he is at asking indirect questions."

"But if he gets a little mixed up it would be much more fun," said the schoolteacher.

"And then how would you want him to guess what it is, smartaleck?" asked the hot-shot. "You just wait till you're the one asking questions."

"All right, let's go on," said the draftsman's wife.

"Is it in the recreation center building?" continued the draftsman, and then with several practiced questions he determined what the object was. To someone new at the game it looked almost like clairvoyance, but it was simply the result of logic and experienced instinct. All the same, some were surprised.

"You really are clever, Mr. N.!" exclaimed the store manager's wife.

"It's not cleverness," the draftsman replied modestly, "you just have to ask the right questions, from the general down to the specific, and in a little while you've got it."

Then it was the hot-shot's turn. I suggested as a subject Louis Armstrong's trumpet. Some voices were raised in opposition — the store manager's wife because she didn't know who Armstrong was, and the schoolteacher who didn't know either — but my suggestion was accepted in the end all the same. I had to answer most of the questions myself.

The road to success was not an easy one for the hot-shot's foggy mind, but once he had determined the approximate size of the object and had ingeniously asked whether you could use it for something, and then thought of asking if it was in Czechoslovakia and then if it was on the earth, and after the third question in this series (Was it in America? since in addition to Czechoslovakia, where he was obliged to live, and the earth, where we are all obliged to live, he knew and loved and was interested in just one other place in the world) he was suddenly inspired or perhaps the focus of his interests suggested the question and he asked if it was used to play on. As soon as he was told that it was, he was home free. By precise reasoning, resulting from his scale of values and his devotion to this love that was, apart from himself, his sole *raison d'être,* he determined that it was a brass instrument, that this instrument was the property of an outstanding jazz musician, that this musician was black, and then victoriously but also piously he pronounced the name, the whole name, as if he were pronouncing a long and awe-inspiring royal title: Louis Satchmo Dippermouth Armstrong.

I looked at the schoolteacher. He glanced at his watch and was silent. When the hot-shot made his guess, the schoolteacher suggested hoarsely that we play something else.

"Oh, no you don't," said the hot-shot insolently. "Not until everybody gets a turn!"

"Yes," said the wife of the clothing-store manager.

"And how about your taking a turn now, Mrs. M.?" said the draftsman's wife.

"Who, me?" asked the wife of the store manager.

"Well?"

"But I don't know how!" exclaimed the fat lady.

"But it's easy," said the draftsman's wife. "You'll catch on."

"Oh, golly, I'll never get it!" said the fat lady and raised her hands to her lips. "Oh, gosh, I don't know how!" She shook her head in the panic of simple women, inexorably convinced they are dumb, ignorant of the wisdom of life that is in them. Everyone started to persuade her. The fat lady kept shaking her head, until finally she began to thaw. "But I don't know," she kept saying, "I won't know what to ask."

"Oh, go on, lady," the hot-shot urged. "We're each as stupid as the next one here, right?" He turned to me.

I laughed and looked at the schoolteacher. He had not joined in the persuading. "Oh, go ahead, Mrs. M.," I said. "Nothing's going to happen to you."

"Well, if you say so," said the store manager's wife rising with difficulty, and with difficulty pressed her way between the knees in the compartment and went outside. Through the glass door, you could see her broad, benign and sweetly simple face puckered in an effort to catch something of the conversation inside.

The group in the compartment decided on a sack of coffee that the lady's husband told us she had in her suitcase. The manager's wife was let in, she giggled, sat down heavily, and opened her mouth.

After much visible effort, she asked, "Wha — what is it?"

"You can't ask like that, Mrs. M. You have to ask questions like my husband did, or Mr. P. here," said the draftsman's wife, nodding toward the hotshot.

"But I don't know how, like that," implored the fat lady.

"Come on. Try it. Slowly," the draftsman's wife soothed her. The fat lady concentrated. Beads of sweat formed on her oily skin and ran down her round cheeks, and after a long moment of intense effort, she blurted out, "Is it here?"

"See how easy it is," said the draftsman's wife. "Yes, it's here in the compartment."

The fat lady looked around. Her little eyes, half

lost in the simple face, so simple that the simplicity was almost a decoration, drifted from object to object, from person to person, rested on the hot-shot's yellow-and-black leather suitcase, the portable radio of the draftsman's wife, the introverted face of the factory foreman, my nylon socks, and finally on the pale face of the schoolteacher, who glared back venomously.

"Is it — is it something to eat?"

"Yes!" exclaimed the chorus. The manager's wife smiled happily.

"So I guessed it!" she said.

"Yes," said the draftsman's wife, "but you still have to keep on guessing."

"How come?" wondered the fat lady.

"So far, you've only guessed the nature of the thing, but you still don't know what it is."

"What nature?" said the manager's wife, bewildered.

"Like you know it's something to eat, but like you don't know what it is," explained the hot-shot.

"Ah," said the lady and looked around again. "But there isn't anything to eat here."

"It doesn't have to be something you can see, does it?" said the draftsman. "It can be put away somewhere."

"But how am I supposed to guess it if it's put away somewhere?" asked the fat lady.

"That's why you've got to ask questions," said the draftsman's wife.

"Questions?"

"That's right. You have to find out exactly where in the compartment it is."

"Exactly?" The wife of the clothing-store manager looked pleadingly at the draftsman's wife.

"Well, you have to find out if it's on the floor or on the seat or in the luggage rack —"

"Is it in a suitcase?" the manager's wife interrupted her.

"It is!" came the chorus.

"So it's doughnuts!" exclaimed the fat lady delightedly. Whereupon she was shattered to discover that she was mistaken. Then she named the edible contents of her suitcase item by item, disregarding protests that you can't ask direct questions, until she guessed it. She glowed with pride. "I guessed it," she said blissfully, and cast her ingenuous smile on the entire company.

"You see!" said the draftsman's wife. The fat lady clasped her husband's arm and said, "Goodness, this game is fun!"

My moment had come. It was as if I could feel Emöke's presence, somewhere in another train compartment and yet almost here, sitting terribly alone, surrounded and harassed again by the spirits of chalk circles, returning to the world of her past, to the fearful solitude of that Hungarian ultima Thule, condemned there forever to the superstitions of the consumptive gardener and to nightmares of the owner of the hotel and farm. I said, "And now the schoolteacher here could take his turn."

The schoolteacher winced. He objected. He said he had never played the game. He even said he wasn't interested but that turned everyone against him. Finally he had to leave, grumbling, and wait behind the glass with his vacant face and his out-thrust lower lip, his dull mean eyes. We agreed on him as the subject. An old trick, easy to guess. This time no one protested. We nodded to him. The schoolteacher came inside.

"Well, what is it?" he said, trying to evoke an impression of jocularity.

"Come on, just ask questions the way you're supposed to," said the store manager's wife.

The schoolteacher sat down. I could sense the gears grinding in his brain accustomed to processing ready-made bits of information and to the endless, fruitless contemplation of ways and means of achieving physical satisfaction. He was incapable of anything. Incapable of the simplest logic. I knew it.

"Is it . . . a house?" he squeezed out of himself. The others, not as well acquainted with him as I, were embarrassed. They didn't know if the schoolteacher was still joking. I knew he was stupid.

"Quit kidding and play it right," the hot-shot said after a pause.

The schoolteacher began to sweat. His black pupils mirrored an inner effort that was more than the organism was used to.

"Is it . . ." he said slowly, "or . . . is it a train?"

"Come on, mister," the hot-shot was irritated, "what d'you think you're doing? Ask right, will you?"

The schoolteacher flushed with fury.

"What do you think I'm doing?" he said, and his eyes flashed with the yearning to be able to exert his schoolroom authority over this conceited puppy in striped socks who was scarcely older than the particular breed of human beings he was used to having in his absolute power.

"You're not doing what you're supposed to be doing," said the hot-shot. "You're asking stupid questions. You can't ask plain out, like is it a dumb-bell or is it a crumb-bun. You have to ask is it like this or that, is it here or there, and like that, don't you see?"

"Is it here or there?" the schoolteacher asked quickly.

"For cripes' — " the hot-shot began, but the draftsman's wife interrupted him.

"It's like this. You can only ask questions that we can answer 'Yes' or 'No' to, do you understand?"

"Naturally," said the schoolteacher. Everyone fell silent. The silence dragged on. The schoolteacher was floundering in embarrassment.

"Come on!" exclaimed the store manager's wife anxious to get on with the game in which she had been so successful.

The schoolteacher rolled his eyes. "Is it something to eat?" he said.

Everyone burst out laughing and the schoolteacher flushed again. This time it was apparent that he was offended.

"No!" exclaimed the two women.

"Sure it is," said the hot-shot.

"How come?" demanded the fat lady.

"Sure it is. Like there are people in the world as would eat it too."

"Yes, but we can't use that," said the draftsman's wife, "because it isn't customary here."

"So what?" said the hot-shot. "So what if we don't eat it here. He asked is it something to eat and I say it is, like if they can eat it in Borneo, it's something to eat, isn't it?"

I observed the schoolteacher. His gaze was flitting from face to face, in complete confusion. His cheeks seemed to have swollen with rage. The dispute between the hot-shot and the draftsman's wife continued. The schoolteacher squirmed and said, "I give up, then."

"Oh, but you can't do that!" squealed the fat lady.

"Why not?" said the schoolteacher. "You don't even know if it's something to eat or not."

"That's 'cause we never tasted it, right?" said the hot-shot. "Maybe it's tough, or maybe it tastes awful and you might get sick to your stomach." I noticed his voice held something more than its usual sing-song intonation; it seemed to contain hatred for the schoolteacher, probably the legacy of years of being derided by some similar member of the teaching profession for his ostentatious adherence to brightly colored clothing, and total self-indulgence as the only possible way of life (whereas his teacher — kindred to this one, paunchy, with soft hands, and a covert lecherousness of mind — would naturally have preached the importance of the work ethic).

"It's like this," the factory foreman interjected (until then he had been silent; in his youth he probably hadn't assimilated much of that negligible store of information that the schoolteacher peddled for a decent month's salary, perhaps he hadn't even finished school and had had to work all his life to make a living, but every day in his few free hours he found time to think, perhaps he read — books of nonfiction, nature, travel; a slow man without too much of a sense of humor but capable of honest logical thought and lacking only in words). "It's like this, sir," he said. "Where we live, it is not eaten, but there are countries of the world where some people might eat it. That's how it is."

The schoolteacher focused his baleful gaze on this new enemy who spoke to him with respect, a respect for the teaching profession and for a teacher's erudition, wisdom, and justice that he had acquired from his elderly parents in his childhood and had passed on to his own children. But the schoolteacher was disdainful.

"I give up," he said again, wearily.

"Don't do that," said the draftsman's wife. "It isn't hard at all."

"No, I give up. It doesn't make sense for me to guess if you think up things that you don't even know if they're something to eat," said the schoolteacher. Once more they tried to persuade him. The fat lady was close to weeping in her impatient pleasure in the game. The schoolteacher, almost black with rage by now, finally gave in and immersed himself again in fruitless thought. It had the external form of something almost Aristotelian, but it was nothing but the gray, impotent pounding of a sledgehammer on an empty anvil.

"Is it . . . a car?" he finally came up with.

The hot-shot broke into a rude laugh. "Are you stupid or something?" Everything that he felt for the schoolteacher burst out of him, openly and directly, without restraint, with the supreme honesty that is perhaps the sole virtue of young hot-shots such as he, apart from a strong fidelity to an ideal. "You ever hear of anybody eating a car, for cripes' sake?"

"Watch your language, you!" the schoolteacher snapped at him.*

"C'mon," said the hot-shot, "you don't have to be so touchy. I didn't say anything all that bad, did I?"

"I'm not playing," said the schoolteacher, indignantly making it clear that he was offended. "I don't have to let myself be insulted."

Supported by a new wave of protest, I entered the fray. "Look," I said, "it's just a matter of thinking your questions over, logically, understand?"

The schoolteacher stabbed me with his eyes. "I said I'm not playing," he repeated.

"But that would be a shame," squealed the manager's wife. "You wouldn't want a disgrace like that!" She had characterized the situation precisely, she was still a little child who couldn't see the Emperor's new clothes.

"Let our friend here explain it to you," said the draftsman's wife, indicating me. "You don't want to be a spoilsport."

---

* The hot-shot has used a Czech synonym for "eat" that in polite language refers only to animals.

The schoolteacher muttered something under his breath.

"You have to start from general terms," I said, "and get increasingly specific as your questions give you more information, understand?"

The schoolteacher didn't say anything.

"Do you see?" I said sweetly. "Start out with something very general, the best is to localize the subject, and then get more and more specific until you determine, shall I say, the exact coordinates." I glanced at him. He didn't understand at all. "The best of all is to find out at the very outset whether it is abstract or concrete."

The schoolteacher was silent.

"So try it. Pose an initial inquiry," I babbled, "and try to localize the subject."

The schoolteacher moved his lips in hatred. "Is . . . is it black?" he said.

The hot-shot guffawed, laughed so hard his spidery legs lifted off the floor and nearly kicked the schoolteacher in the nose.

"That is a very specific premise," I prattled affably, "and it cannot tell you anything about the localization. Localize, localize!" I kept on.

"Is it . . ." said the teacher dully, "is it a train carriage?"

"Ah, no, it's not." I raised my eyebrows. "And that doesn't tell you anything about the localization either."

The hot-shot whinnied. "Dammit, so ask where it is already!"

The schoolteacher glared at him. "I asked already."

"Yeah, but how! You can't ask 'Is it here or there?' " he mimicked — very successfully — the inane melody of the schoolteacher's questions. "You have to say 'Is it here?' or 'Is it . . . is it . . .' " he searched his mind quickly for something clever. The only thing that occurred to him was what to his comrades, and many others, is the epitome of all humor. "Is it up your ass, maybe?"

"But Mr. P.!" giggled the wife of the clothing-store manager.

"I'm not playing," said the schoolteacher. "I don't play with people who don't know anything about polite behavior," he declared virtuously.

But he did play. They forced him to, and it lasted all the way to Pardubice, where he and the manager of the clothing store got off. It was the greatest fun that this parlor game had ever given me or the hot-shot or the wife of the draftsman, because it wasn't fun, it was the mill of God grinding him between its stone wheels. Slowly, with an immense series of silly questions that finally lost all semblance of system, he got himself into the mental state known in boxing circles as "punch-drunk." With questions like "Does it stink?" he elicited a remarkable and copious flow of sarcasm from the soul of the hot-shot, whose brightly colored socks rose more and more frequently like fireworks toward the ceiling. With the question "Is it anything at all?" he gave me food for thought, because I truly didn't know what it was, this schoolteacher, lifelong proclaimer of a morality that was founded on no law whatsoever, not Christ's, not Marx's, and himself living without morality, without even the morality of a human animal which recognizes the ageless law of the herd — don't do things you don't want people to do to you — living a life without meaning or content, a mere system of bowels and reflexes, more pitiful than a silky little hamster caught in a cage, trying in vain with its pink claws to dig its way out through the metal cage floor, to the only thing of value — sweet freedom. This creature here didn't need freedom, which is certainly of supreme value in our life but cannot be achieved except in the wisdom that understands our necessity, even though he often spouted the word "freedom" at Party meetings; he didn't need the freedom that we need to remain sane if we are human beings, because he wasn't human. Naturally there is no such thing as a superman, but it always seemed to me that there is such a thing as a subman. He exists, he is among us for all the days of the world, like Jesus's poor, except that the submen aren't poor. Small or large, fat or skinny mammals unfamiliar with love, fidelity, honesty, altruism — all those virtues and attributes that make up a human being and justify the survival of the species of animals and men (conscious in humans, unconscious in animals, in armadillos, or white mice that in their natural state would never in all their short lives think of killing each other) — who with no qualms assert the absolute priority of their bellies, their imagined (but to them indisputable) rights, and broadcast their own inanity in speeches about their infallibility, always ready to judge others, to condemn others, not for an instant doubting their own perfection, not for a moment contemplating the meaning of their own existence, deriding Christianity and morality as outdated but in the depths of their souls hating Communism, which robs them of the freedom to be parasites, although some occasionally even win out over that because they find they can sponge off it equally well, and they never realize that they are simply a terrible emptiness bounded by skin and bone, leaving in their wake traces of lesser or greater pain, ruined lives, wrecked existences, jobs spoiled, tasks undone, wretched divorces, crimes, and dull and sordid cynicism. They are the ones for whom hell and eternal punishment must exist, at least the punishment of human memory, if everything in the world is not to become one immense injustice, because perhaps not even the entire future of Communism-come to pass can make up for the oceans of suffer-

ing they have precipitated upon the world in the
eight or nine thousand years of their existence, for
the subhumans have always succeeded in accom-
modating themselves while others suffered, have
always been quick to advocate Truths, for they are
indifferent to truth, insidiously forging pain in the
hearts of betrayed friends, mauled wives, deserted
mistresses, battered children, destroyed competitors
who stood in their way, victims of their mean hatred
which needs no motive, only blood, only revenge
cruel and direct or dressed in the juridical verdict
of a juridical society. Yes, they are among us still,
more so than Jesus's poor, like an evil reproach and
a derision of our pretty words, like a memento of
our conceit, a warning to the peace of our self-
satisfaction.

Finally the factory foreman took pity on the
schoolteacher, and using his ordinary common
sense and patient simplicity led him to the humiliat-
ing mark: to the recognition that the object of his
quest was himself, that it was his own person that
was the inane answer to the collection of idiotic
questions he had posed and that cost him the greatest humiliation of his life, or whatever it was he
lived. He got off at Pardubice, and didn't even say
goodbye to me.

That was my revenge. But then, when I arrived in Prague and strode with the crowd down the underground corridor of the railway station toward the exit where clusters of girls' faces awaited me, powdered and delicate, beautiful Prague faces, and when the motley, somber streets took me into their noisy gullets, brightened by the colorful bells of full-skirted summer dresses and hemmed in by the racket of everyday disagreements, when I met again, furtively, with Margit in her blue-and-white striped dress at a discreet booth-table at Myšák's Café, Margit, who lived on crème caramel and turned to me with tender amorous eyes, when I began again to take part in that great game of petty cruelties, artifices, pretenses and lies born of a longing for a paradise lost, for a different, more perfect Man who might once have been and may once again be but is perhaps only just being born by the great and difficult Caesarean section of socialism (or maybe he is toddling around in diapers already in the wake of the factory foreman, but I don't know, I can't tell, I couldn't say), then Emöke was only a dream again, only a legend that perhaps never was, a distant echo of an alien destiny, and soon I had almost ceased to believe in her existence. I didn't write to her, I didn't send her the books I had planned to — philosophy, a short private course in the history of thought from Socrates to Engels — I never went to Košice.

And in time, very quickly, I was permeated with an indifference toward the legend, the indifference that allows us to live in a world where creatures of our own blood are dying every day of tuberculosis and cancer, in prisons and concentration camps, in distant tropics and on the cruel and insane battlefields of an Old World drunk on blood, in the lunacy of disappointed love, under the burden of ludicrously negligible worries, that indifference that is our mother, our salvation, our ruin.

And that is how a story, a legend, comes to pass and no one tells it. And yet, somewhere, someone lives on, afternoons are hot and idle, and the person grows older, is deserted, dies. All that is left is a slab, a name. Maybe not even a slab, not even a name. The story is borne for a few more years by another, and then that person dies too. And other people know nothing, as they never, never, never knew anything. The name is lost. As is the story, the legend. Neither a name nor a memory nor even an empty space is left. Nothing.

But perhaps somewhere at least an impression is left, at least a trace of the tear, the beauty, the loveliness of the person, the legend, Emöke.

I wonder, I wonder, I wonder.

THE BASS SAXOPHONE

TO JOE MEDJUCK

A Friend

Kreischend zögen die Geier Kreise.
Die riesigen Städte stünden leer.
Die Menschheit läg in den Kordilleren.
Das wüsste dann aber keiner mehr.

                    ERICH KÄSTNER

Twilight. Honey and blood. Indifferent to the historical situation of nation and town, it spoke to me, aged eighteen, on the leeshore of a land-locked lea in Europe, where death was less extravagant, more modest. I stood with my back to the *fin de siècle* hotel façade, a product of that time when they exerted their strained imaginations to create something entirely new, something they couldn't express through classical form and to which they gave instead an expression of ineptitude that is actually beautiful when you get right down to it, being a reflection of man's image of man rather than an effort to copy God. Anyway, there I stood, my back to that hotel façade with the greenish mosaic around the big windows of the hotel café, windows with flowers etched in the glass, while dusk, a puddle of honey, trickled down the wall.

At first I didn't even realize that that was what the thing was. Not until the old man in the shabby jacket made of a wartime cellulose ersatz material (it was wartime) dragged it out of the little gray bus, and as he strained to pick it up the clasps loosened and the big black case opened before it was high enough off the ground for what was inside to fall out; it opened an inch or two above the pavement, so that all that really happened was that the case opened a crack and the light of the honey-colored sun (standing over the tubby tower of the town's old mansion, blazing in through the windows of the square tower of the town's new mansion that belonged to Domanín, the millionaire whose daughter I was in love with because she lived in that tower and every night all the points of the compass caught the light of her alabaster lamp shining through the four aquariums, and she was pale, pale, she was ill in that world of purple fish, just another illusion, just a pathological dream of a pathological childhood) glinted on the immense, incredible bell of a bass saxophone, as big around as a washbasin.

I had never actually believed that such things really existed. I only knew they had been mentioned back in the days of Dadaism and Poetism; maybe some time in the ancient history of the republic somebody made a museum piece like that, an advertising gimmick, too expensive really and later stored away in some forgotten back room. And after that nobody made them any more, they were only a dream, a theoretical computation formulated some time in the colorful twenties: all we had were alto saxes and tenor saxes. And way up in the hills, in Rohelnice, there lived a fellow named Syrovátka, son of a country schoolteacher who led the village brass band, and he was the possessor of a legendary baritone sax; he used to play alto sax with village bands in a sweet uncertain tone; he didn't swing, he was a country boy, all the way. But he possessed an old baritone sax, an instrument blind with decay and verdigris, stored away in the hills in the loft of a thatch-roofed cottage where the gleam of the ruby sun penetrated through holes in the roof. To this very day, I can see the poisonous turquoise sky above the black smudge of the woods; in it floats that bloodshot eye, a red olive floating in greenish-blue wine — evening in the hills, reminiscent of times Paleozoic and of fern jungles — its light penetrating through cracks in the thatched roof to the muggy silver of the mastodon corpus. In 1940, when the unbelievable became possible (six brasses, a big band, bass, percussion, guitar, piano), Syrovátka came down from the hills and then it was five saxes; in his jacket made of flour sacking, he sat at the very end of the white row, his shoulders like the front of an angular chest of drawers; no, he didn't swing, but the mythical instrument gave off a dull sheen in the glow of the footlights, and above it the four of us sang, sang for joy that he was with us even though he was striding his own hill and forest paths under our sliding chords. But this thing here, this was something even more mysterious: a bass saxophone. (Perhaps the significance of things like that is beyond belief — things like a barely used and hardly usable instrument in the eyes of a complex-ridden kid in the middle of Europe, surrounded by names that were to become entries in hell's own dictionary: Maidanek, Auschwitz, Treblinka. But what are we permitted to choose in this life of ours? Nothing. Everything comes to us willy-nilly.)

It was revealed to me for an instant, a silvery fish in that bubble of honey called Indian summer; I stared at it the way a child stares at its first doll. But it only lasted an instant — the old man in the wood-pulp jacket bent over, his joints creaking aloud with rheumatism, the rheumatism of war begotten from sleeping on benches in railway stations. He bent down and shut the lid; he started to tie the broken lock with a piece of string.

I said, "Good evening." I asked, "Mister, is that a bass saxophone?" It wasn't that I didn't know, but I wanted to be told; I wanted to talk about it; I'd never even heard what it sounded like, only read about it in a finger-marked old book that Benno had, that he'd swiped from one of his play-boy Jewish uncles in Prague — and besides, the book was in French, a language I refused to study, so our French teacher had declared me a remark-able anti-talent (for I was secretly using the time to study the language of blues from a cheap little brochure) — called *Le Jazz Hot,* which the playboy Jewish uncle had bought somewhere in Paris and brought back to Prague, and that's when Benno stole it to take home to Kostelec, our town. Now, like the Book of Mormon of origin divine, it was shelved in the leather-bound library of Benno's father in the huge villa by the river in that little provincial town in the middle of Europe, in the middle of the war; like the Book of Mormon written in the language of angels, it spoke to me only in the language of objects (bass saxophone, sarrusophone, cowbells, mellophone) and people (Trixie Smith, Bix Beiderbecke, Bud Freeman, Johnny St. Cyr) and places (Storyville, Canal Street, Milneburg) and bands (Condon's Chicagoans, the Wolverines, the Original Dixieland Band), that international language of an innocent cult . . . Adrian Rollini — only a name, a bass saxophone player from Chicago whom I'd never heard play — I knew only that he was occasionally a member of that good old gang that used to make recordings into acoustic funnels.

The old man straightened up and his joints complained again. The material on his knees sagged. His scalp was crumpled like the shell of a boiled egg that had burst; one eye sat lower than the other, almost down on his cheek, a bluish eye, surrounded by fair whiskers. *"Verstehe nicht tschechisch,"* he said. His other, healthier eye moved, slid down my checkered jacket to my hand which was clutching a folder with a label on it that said "2nd Ten. Sax." So I repeated my question in German. *"Ist das ein Bassaxophon, bitte?"* That very act alone removed me from the Czech community, since German was only spoken under duress; at the first sound of German I should have turned on my heel and gone away, bid the bass saxophone goodbye. But some things are simply stronger. So I said *"Ist das ein Bassaxophon, bitte?"* and the eye, not the bluish one, the healthier one, rested on my folder and then slowly, searchingly, with a certain degree of contempt, it rose again, past my checkered jacket, skimmed the black shoestring under my short collar, bounced off the broad brim of my porkpie hat (I was a dandy, oh, yes, I was; it had its political significance too — foppery is always a calling card of the opposition — but not only that: it also had something to do with the myth, the myth of youth, that myth of myths) and looked right at me. It examined me. *"Ja,"* the old man said. *"Das ist es. Du spielst auch Saxophon?"* He used the familiar *"Du"* when he asked me if I could play; it didn't even appear particularly strange.

"Ja," I said. *"Sie auch?* You too?" But the old man didn't reply. He bent over again. The same creaking, cracking sound as if every move meant a crumbling, a breaking of his skeleton shattered to

little tiny bonelets by some kind of dumdum — but what held him together then? Probably just will power, the will power that is in the ones who survive all the explosions, apparently only to die not long afterward; everything in them is worn away, cracked: liver, lungs, kidneys, and soul. He untied the string with stained fingers. They trembled. The coffin opened, and there it lay, big as a bishop's staff. And the old man creaked again, and again he looked at me. I was staring at the bass saxophone, at its long incredible body, the high metal loop on top; it was dim and blinded, like the baritone sax in Rohelnice. These instruments were mere vestiges of older, better, happier days and it was a long time since they had manufactured any; all they made now was *Panzerschrecks,* bazookas, simply plates of rolled steel. *"Möchtest du's spielen?"* asked the old man like the Serpent. Would I like to play it? Yes, because it was the apple and I was Eve; or else he was a miserable, hideous Eve with one bad eye in a golden wreath of whiskers, and I was Adam. I suddenly remembered something about nationality and patriotism, and my humanity was diminished by that something; I heard the voice of reason, that idiotic voice, saying, when all is said and done, it's only a musical instrument, and this is a Czech town called Kostelec. The child fell silent, the doll closed its eyes; I was eighteen years old, I was grown up. I looked at the old man, at the ugly Eve, and my glance slipped to one side to the little gray bus. Somewhere, on an ostentatious glass-covered Nazi Party bulletin board, I had happened to see a notice that Lothar Kinze and his Entertainment Orchestra would be coming to town, and that's what the weatherbeaten letters on the gray bus said: LOTHAR KINZE MIT SEINEM UNTER-HALTUNGSORCHESTER; and it had said on that glass-covered bulletin board that it would be a *Konzert für die deutsche Gemeinde in Kosteletz,* in other words a concert for the local Nazis, for the ones that had been here all along (Herr Zeeh, Herr Trautner, Herr Pellotza-Nikschitsch) and the Nazi office workers that had migrated here from the Reich in order to recuperate in the safety of the Protectorate of Bohemia and Moravia, and for the air force radio men from the Ernst Udet Barracks, and also for Mr. Kleinenherr, who didn't give a damn about nationality either, and kept right on associating with the Czechs and speaking Czech. For Germans only. Czechs prohibited. So I took them up on it, and played the game. Instead of killing with kindness (love your enemies, do good unto those that hate you) I tried responding with hatred. But there was no hatred in me; certainly no hatred toward this old man with his eyes on crooked, not even toward the *Feldwebel,* the sergeant-major (or whatever his rank was) from the Ernst Udet Barracks who used to hang around my sister as doggedly as a faithful bull terrier when she walked home from work at the brewery office; he would always say hello and she, like the good Czech that she was, would always walk a little faster, and yet that *Feldwebel* had sad, German eyes under the foreign cap with the eagle and the swastika, eyes of yearning in a gaunt, expressionless Prussian countenance, but my sister was a good Czech, and besides, she was afraid of him; more that than anything else — my sister was a good girl; and once I saw him sitting by the weir, the Ledhuje river murmuring, the weeping willows whispering, gray clouds marching toward the black east; he sat there, his boots in the grass, writing something in a blue pocket-notebook; I sneaked up to the weir and through a knothole watched the hand with the pencil, and I read a few German words in a Gothic script: *"Bald kommen Winterstürme mit dem roten Schneen. O Anna, komm zu mir den grausam gelben Pfad! In meinem Kopfe kalte Winde wehen."* I never saw him again after that, his platoon or his company or whatever he belonged to was shipped to the front shortly afterward, but my sister's name was Anna and on either side of the road from the brewery there were horse chestnut trees that turned yellow at the end of summer, turned orange and finally died, leaving only the black skeletons of the trees behind. But all the same, I shook my head, all the same I turned on my heel. Old Mr. Káňa was standing in front of the church with the onion-shaped tower, watching me (another time, two years earlier, it had been old Mr. Vladyka who had stood there and he had watched me too as I tried to convince Mr. Katz, the teacher, that it would all turn out all right; there is always a Mr. Káňa or a Mr. Vladyka watching you from somewhere unless you do nothing and are nothing, and perhaps even then; they follow us from the time it's possible to punish us, or to punish our parents through us, or our acquaintances, or our close friends; maybe we'll never get rid of those stares, that hell of ours: the others). I started to walk away; I felt the old man's hand fall on my shoulder. It was like the touch of an iron claw, but gentle, not the hand of the Gestapo, just the hand of a soldier, for there is a gentleness in the hands of the skeletons called to arms under those flags of theirs; particularly when they return defeated, and for those skeletons it can never be anything other than defeat. *"Warte mal,"* I heard his voice, it sounded like two voices, two cracked vocal chords split lengthwise in two. "Can't you give me a hand? This damned giant saxophone is too heavy for me." I stopped. Mr. Káňa took a cigarette case out of his pocket, and lit himself a cigarette. The old man's crippled eyes stared at me as if they were gazing out of some terrible fairy tale; but at his feet, in a black coffin with faded velvet cushioning, rested a bass saxophone. The child reopened its eyes. The doll spoke. Little suns rested for an instant on the valves of the huge corpus, valves as big as the ornaments on a horse's trappings. "*Ja, Bassaxophon,*" said the old man. "Have you ever heard it played? It has a voice like a bell. *Sehr traurig.* Very sad." The creaking of those vocal chords made me think of the *Feldwebel* again, writing poems in a pocket-notebook on the bank of the Ledhuje, of that one-man unit lost in the immensity of the war, like a clumsy tortoise running up against the shield of my sister's lack of understanding, of that man, undoubtedly alone amongst the men in uniform (it wasn't an SS barracks, it was just an ordinary German barracks; but even if it had been an SS barracks, who knows? the roads of our lives lead heaven knows where); we will certainly never see him again, neither I nor my sister; I gazed at that sad instrument, and in my mind the unknown Adrian Rollini rose up behind the wire music stand of years past, sad as a bell. The doll fell silent again. "Excuse me," I said. "I'm in a hurry." And then I turned away again, in order to save myself in the last moment from treason, in the eyes of Mr. Káňa, but the iron hand of the skeleton held me fast. "*Nein,* you can't go," said the voice, and his face suddenly assumed a mask; it was only a mask, and from beneath it the uncertain countenance of a problem showed through — what it was, I didn't know. "You will help me carry the saxophone!" I wanted to jerk myself free, but just then an immense man in uniform walked out of the door of the hotel, spread his legs and turned his yellow face to the sun; it gleamed like a big puddle of lemon, two gray eyes opened in it, like Nosferatu gazing out of his lemony grave. "No, I can't, really, let me go," I said, and moved abruptly so the old man almost lost his footing, but he held fast. *"Herr Leutnant!"* he called; the gray eyes looked at me; I was trying to pull free; from the corner of my eye, I saw Mr. Káňa standing at a safe distance and it seemed to me that he nodded in approval; the old man was saying something to the man with a face like Nosferatu. Not voluntarily, then; if they force me though, it's all right. "Why don't you want to help him?" asked the lieutenant. "He's an old man, after all. *Ein alter Mann.*" I looked up at him; he was huge, but sad, just a facsimile of a soldier; the gray eyes rested in his intelligent countenance like the Arnheim eggs. "And you are both musicians," he said. "Help him with the saxophone." I picked it up. The iron hand released me. I threw the black coffin onto my shoulder and started out behind the old man. I wondered whether this great big meaty fellow had a notebook too. Possibly, probably. He didn't shout; he didn't give any orders. "You are both musicians."

So I carried the bass saxophone through the

hotel lobby, which looked very different from the way it had when I was there last. I entered another world. I wasn't in Kostelec any more: red flags with a white and black picture of an evil sun, the bronze bust of *that* fellow (after the war, when we smashed it, it turned out not to be of bronze at all, but papier-mâché); a lady in a dirndl at the reception desk; a couple of soldiers. I carried the bass saxophone in its black case past them — it had nothing to do with Germans or non-Germans, it was from the twenties; *that* fellow was nothing in those days.

Then up the coco-fiber runner to the second floor. A beige corridor, another world again. A small-town dream of luxury. Brass numbers on cream-colored doors, and silence. A sharp German voice sliced into the silence from behind one of the doors.

The old man — I had just noticed that he limped and was dragging what remained of one foot behind him; not that there was a piece of his foot missing, but every time he stepped down on his other, healthy foot, the sick foot didn't raise itself from the ground but dragged behind, the sole cross-wise, scraping along the carpet, sweeping up dust until he put his weight on it again — took hold of the handle of the door labeled 12A (how splendidly secure must have been the era that was afraid to put a brass thirteen on this cream-colored door, afraid that it might lose a customer because the guest, perhaps the owner of a car, certainly a well-to-do fellow if he could use the services of the local hotel, might refuse to sleep behind that unlucky number and instead climb into his car and ride off into the safety of the night, to the competitors in the neighboring town, to another cream-colored room, to another vain, long-since forgotten night, forgotten like all of them have been forgotten; and only the number, 12A, has remained) and opened it. He maneuvered me with the bass saxophone through the door, and I immediately began to wonder. Why here? Why to a boudoir with gilded furniture? This kind of big instrument didn't belong here, it belonged in dressing rooms behind a stage, somewhere near the auditorium in the rear of the hotel. Then why here? Was this some kind of trick? A trap? But the old man had already closed the door, and that was when I saw the man on the gilded bed, or rather, his head; he was lying under the blue and white hotel blanket, breathing soundlessly through his open mouth, his eyes shut. The room shone like a yellow-gold lantern, the sun of early autumn reaching its yellow rays through the curtains. It was something like the old engravings: a baroque sun glinting on the amazed witnesses to a vision (the only thing missing was a naïve madonna and a falling housepainter saved by the madonna invoked at the right moment); but it was no vision, if you don't count the fossil instrument hidden in the im-

mense case, it was just a man on a gilded bed, a
head with an open mouth, the breath gently rattling
through a throat recently scorched by the icy winds
of the Eastern Front and the sands of El Alamein,
and other towns deep in the desert with names that
might have been invented by the Poetist poets, with
structures of bleached bones and sand-smoothed
helmets that some new Hieronymus Bosch will use
to weave the frames for neo-baroque paintings in
the forthcoming dark age; and behind the gentlest
of all rattles was the afternoon silence of the siesta,
the light from the round brass lamps on the night
table that didn't match the bed, and a pink painting
of a pink girl holding a pink cherub that could have
been meant to be Jesus Christ, and silence; and in
that silence another, distant, brittle but dangerous,
spitting voice. I turned to the old man; the fellow
on the bed didn't move; one of the old man's eyes
was staring at me, but it was the blind one, the one
on his cheek, the other was listening to the sound
of the distant voice; and then I realized that it
wasn't distant, that it was only behind the wall and
that it was indeed menacingly close. Once again I
looked at the old man, at his other eye; it supported
my impression of the danger of that voice. Not
fright, just apprehension; the old man (a survivor
of Armageddon) was beyond all fear, he had seen
too much of death, he was indifferent to it, and what
else is there to be afraid of if not death or pain (and

he had experienced pain greater than the proximity
of death)? So it could only be a look of apprehension, a sort of anxiety. "Well, goodbye," I said,
and turned to go; the old man stretched out a hand
that looked like a root. "Wait!" he snapped, and
kept on listening, he hadn't for a moment stopped
listening, to that mad midget voice behind the wall.
Ten seconds passed, thirty seconds; perhaps a minute. "I have to . . ." But the rootlike hand waved,
impatiently, angrily. I looked at the case holding
the bass saxophone. It too bore traces of old age;
it had decorative metalwork on the corners, like
the plush-bound family chronicle that my grand-
mother used to have.

"You may take a look at it," croaked the split
vocal chords — the old man's not the fellow's behind the wall, whose vocal chords were just fine
(their owner lived off his vocal chords; if he were
to lose them, get tumors on them or find them occupied by colonies of TB germs, it would be the end,
he wouldn't survive his voice, for the voice *an sich*
was his livelihood, his social position; only the
voice was important, not the brain in which the
voice had its center; such voices are not controlled
by the brain, such voices control themselves and
their centers). The old man's voice said, "You may
take a look at it. Or even try it out, if you want to."
I looked at him. His eye was no longer listening to

the voice. It was looking at me, almost kindly, *"Ja,"* I said, "I'd like to, but . . ." and I looked at the metalwork decorations, I opened the case. The baroque rays of light caressed the corpus, the washbasin full of verdigris and the dried spit of bar musicians. *"Ja,"* I said, *"das ist sensationell."* I translated my supreme recognition verbatim. I reached inside the case and raised it the way I would help a sick friend to sit up. And it rose in front of me. A mechanism of strong, silver-plated wires, the gears, the levers, like the mechanism of some huge and absolutely nonsensical apparatus, the fantasy of some crazy mixed-up inventor. It stood in my hand like the tower of Babel, a conical shape, the valves reflecting my face full of respect, hope, and love — and faith (it was ridiculous, I know, but love is always ridiculous, like faith: the mechanism interested me more than any philosophy ever had, and I admired it more than any Venus possible — certainly more than the Venuses of Kostelec's town square, and certainly more than any other, say the Venus de Milo; a rarely used and almost unusable instrument, a nightmare of any instrument maker, a curious jest of some man long since dead, possessed by the idea of piston trumpets and metal clarinets); it sounds ridiculous, absurd, monstrous, but the thing was beautiful. It stood like a blind silver tower, submerged in a golden sea, in a beige and gold room in a town hotel, touched by timid fingers, and behind it Rollini's ghost at the other end of the world in Chicago.

I looked around; I suddenly felt I was alone (except for the fellow in the bed, but he was asleep), and I was. I lowered the bass saxophone carefully into its plush bed, stepped over to the door and put my hand on the doorknob; it was still warm from the recent touch of a feverish hand; it was a brass hand itself, holding a horizontal stick with a ball on the end. I turned it, but the door didn't open. I was locked in the room that shone like a beige and gold lantern.

I turned back toward all that light. A sleepy autumn fly was circling over the blind, silver torso in the plush coffin. It was humming. It was flying through the cosmic rain of glowing dust particles in the baroque fascia of sunlight; I stepped toward the wall.

The wallpaper was old and stained, but faded pictures of doves still showed against the beige background. I put my ear to their delicate breasts. The voice came close; it was repeating a nasty, unintelligible litany of anger and irritation, of imperious, spit-polished, boot-shod hysterics. I recognized it. I couldn't understand what he was saying, but I knew who it was talking behind the gentle doves in the next, equally beige hotel room: it was Horst Hermann Kühl; it was the same voice that screeching along ahead of him had penetrated all the way up the iron staircase to the roof of the Sokol Hall, where you had to climb down another iron staircase to reach the projection booth of the movie house (I wasn't there at the time, but Mack, who operated the projector, told me about it). A pair of black boots had appeared on the iron rungs, the voice lashing in ahead of them. "What is this supposed to mean?" he had rasped like a poisonous firecracker. "This is a provocation!" Such was the terrific power of that dark voice (not the voice of Horst Hermann Kühl, but the black singer's — they even said it was Ella Fitzgerald, I didn't know, they were old records, Brunswick, before the era of stars, and the label said nothing but "Chick Webb and his Orchestra with Vocal Chorus"; there was a short sobbing saxophone solo — they said that was Coleman Hawkins — and they said the other was Ella Fitzgerald, that voice) it had forced Horst Hermann Kühl, omnipotent within the wartime world of Kostelec, to leave the seat in which he was enjoying the intermission between the newsreel and the film starring Christine Söderbaum or maybe it was Heidemarie Hathayer; when he heard black Ella ("I've got a guy, He don't dress me in sable, He looks nothing like Gable, But he's mine") he flew out of his comfortable seat and squealing like a rutting male mouse (it all took on the dimensions of the microworld of Kostelec) he tore down the aisle between the seats to the lobby and up the steps and up the iron staircase to the roof and down the iron ladder (more ladder than staircase) to the projection booth and, still squealing, confiscated the record and took it away with him. Mack told on me; yes, he did; what was he supposed to do? He could have said he didn't know where the Chick Webb record came from, he could have played stupid, that tried and tested Czech prescription; sometimes they fell for it; they almost loved stupid Schweiks — in contrast, they themselves glowed with vociferous wisdom. But it didn't occur to Mack, so he told on me.

I had committed a crime; it seems unbelievable today what could (can) be a crime: a Beatles haircut in Indonesia (that's today, and that kind of power is always a festering effusion of weakness) — our ducktail haircuts were also once a crime, just like the locks on the heads of youths that shock syphilitic waiters so much today; and the fact that my father had been seen conversing with Mr. Kollitschoner; and the conviction that *Drosophila* flies are suitable for biological experiments; the use of slang; a joke about the president's wife; faith in the miraculous power of paintings and statues; a lack of faith in the miraculous power of paintings and statues; and everywhere the eyes, the spying eyes of the Káňas and the Vladykas; and the ears; and the little reports; and the file cards, keypunched, cybernetic, apparently the first things of all to be cyberneticized. I used to draw advertising slides for the movie house; I would carry them down the iron ladder to the projection booth and because beauty-inspired joy, pleasure-inspired pleasure is diminished by solitude, it had occurred to me: I had those rare records at home, I always used to listen to them before I went to sleep, on an old wind-up phonograph next to my bed: "Doctor Blues," "St. James Infirmary," "Blues in the Dark," "Sweet Sue," the Boswell Sisters, "Mood Indigo," "Jump, Jack, Jump"; and so one day in the projection booth when the electric phonograph was spinning and amplifying a native polka called "Hey, Ma, Who Are You Saving Your Daughter For?" the idea had possessed me: I made my decision. In spite of the fact that they were so rare, I had brought them to the booth (I had labeled the vocal pieces with paper tape so Mack wouldn't make a mistake and put one on by accident) and while _Herr Regierungskommissar_ and the others were awaiting the beginning of the film _"Quax, der Bruchpilot,"_ I was awaiting the first beats of Webb's drum in the foxtrot "Congo" — the annunciation, the sending down of beauty on the heads in the movie house; and when it finally came, that bliss, that splendor, I looked down through the little window and I couldn't understand why no heads were turned, no eyes opened in amazement, that they were not suddenly quiet and that the jaws cracking wartime sour candy did not pause in their effort; the crowd murmured on in their trite crowd conversation; and then, that once, Mack made a mistake (he explained later that the label had come unstuck on that side of the record); the crowd murmured on, ignoring the smeared swinging of Chick's saxes, and murmured on when Ella came in with her nasal twang ("I've got a guy, and he's tough, He's just a gem in the rough, But when I polish him up, I swear . . ."); only Horst Hermann Kühl stopped talking, pricked up his ears, took notice, and then cut loose with a roar (hate is unfortunately always much more observant than love, and more observant even than an insufficiency of love).

I never got that record back; I never found out what happened to it. It disappeared into his five-room apartment, which was built around an altar (yes, an altar) with a life-size portrait of *that* fellow on it; after the war, when we broke in there with a number of other armed musicians, the record wasn't anywhere to be found — only the deserted man in the portrait, and someone who had got there before us had drawn a pince-nez on him and a full beard to go with the mustache, and, along with it, a ridiculously long penis hanging out of his military fly; Horst Hermann Kühl had left town in time, with all his property. Maybe he even took her with him, black Ella, maybe he broke her in a fit of anger, threw her into the ash can. Nothing happened to me; my father set the cogs on the wheels of contacts moving, influence, intercession, advocates, middlemen for bribes, and Kühl simmered down. We belonged among the important people in town (although later, toward the end of the war, they locked my father up for that very reason; in fact he was locked up a number of times for that reason, a position like that is always relative: it can often save you and apparently equally often destroy you, you are always an object of hate, always in the public eye, you can get away with what the populace can't and you can't get away with what the populace can); that's why nothing happened to me and the provocation (arousing public indignation with black Ella's singing in English, while the German citizens of Kostelec were waiting for the romance of Christine Söderbaum) was forgotten. Kühl was silent about it, a silence apparently bought with a bottle of Meinl's rum or something similar (the way payment used to be made in antiquity with cattle, so it is made in the modern world with alcohol: *pecunia — alcunia*).

So I can safely say that I recognized the voice of Horst Hermann Kühl. It was easy, in fact; I had never heard him talk — he was either silent or he was yelling. Now he was yelling, behind the wall covered with beige wallpaper with its faded design of silver doves, and I pressed my ear up against their delicate breasts. What he was yelling was unintelligible. In the passionate beating of his words, like the beating of a dove's heart, I caught fragments that made no sense: ". . . *noch nicht so alt . . . an der Ostfront gibt's keine Entschuldigung . . . jeder Deutsche . . . heute ein Soldat. . . . . . .* not so old yet . . . on the Eastern Front there are no excuses . . . every German . . . today a soldier . . ." His German was entirely different from that of the mournful *Feldwebel*, inscribed in Gothic script in a blue notebook (but there are two tongues within every language: not class tongues, nor does the difference between them have anything to do with the difference between literate language and vulgar slang — the dividing line cuts somewhere down the middle of both); Kühl had mastered only one tongue, like Werner, the School Inspector, who tore past the hall patrol like a cannonball (Lexa, our fourth tenor sax, had an encounter with him once and was the recipient of unwelcome praise; Werner liked opposition), burst into our classroom and started to yell at the frail consumptive professor of German; the professor listened with his head on one side, calmly, with Christian equanimity, perhaps resigned to fate. Werner shouted, ranted and raved, spewing ugly words like *Kerl, Dreck, Schwein,* and *Scheisse;* we didn't understand him but we knew he certainly wasn't praising the professor; the professor listened; when the inspector paused to take a breath, he took advantage of the moment and spoke, gently, quietly but clearly, with dignity, almost reverently. "I teach Goethe's German, *Herr Inspektor,*" he said. "I do not teach pig-German." Amazingly, no apocalyptic storm arose. The Inspector fell silent, visibly deflated, turned on his heel and disappeared. The only thing that remained of him was a diabolical stink of boot polish.

"I don't want to hear a word! I'll be waiting for this evening," then the voice of Horst Hermann Kühl behind the wall lapsed back into hollering incomprehensibility. Someone (behind the wall) tried to say something, but the whiplash of Kühl's high voice silenced him. I stepped away from the doves; the dusty golden fingers of early autumn were still climbing the wallpaper, up a wardrobe with cream-colored angels with peeling golden locks, forming a canopy of stardust over the bass saxophone. The man in the bed was still asleep. His chin jutted up from the pillow like some desperate cliff. It reminded me of the chin of my dead grandfather; his chin had stuck up out of the coffin like that too, with the stubble that outlives a man, as if in derision. But this one was still alive.

And I was at an age when one doesn't think of death. I approached the bass saxophone again. The main part of the body lay to the left, deep in its plush bed. Next to it lay the other sections: the long metal pipe with huge valves for the deepest tones, the bent lever and the little leather-covered plate on the octave valve, the conical end with the big mouthpiece.

They attracted me the way the requisites for mass attract a novice. I leaned over and lifted the body out of its plush bed. Then the second part; I put them together, I embraced the body with gentle fingers, the familiar fingering, my little finger on the ribbed G flat, the valves of the bass thunder deep down under the fingers of my right hand; I wiggled my fingers; the mechanism rattled pleasantly; I pressed down valve after valve, from B all the way to C and then B flat to B with my little finger, and in the immense hollow spaces of the bass saxophone the bubbling echo of tiny leather strokes sounded, descending the scale, like the tiny footsteps of a minute priest in a metal sanctuary, or the drumming of little drums in metal frames, a mysterious telegram of tiny tom-toms; I could not resist, I reached for the mouthpiece, attached it, and opened the plush lid of the little compartment in the corner of the coffin; there they were, a bundle of big reeds, like the shovels bakers use to take bread out of the oven; I stuck one of the reeds in its holder, straightened the edge, and putting the mouthpiece in my mouth, moistened the reed. I didn't play. I just stood there with the mouthpiece in my mouth, my fingers spread and embracing the immense body of the saxophone, my eyes misty; I pressed the big valves. A bass saxophone.

I had never held one in my hands before; I felt as if I were embracing a mistress (Domanín's daughter, that mysterious lily among aquariums, or Irene, who didn't give a damn about me; in fact I couldn't have been happier if I had been holding Irene, or even that girl of the fish and the moon). I stood there, a little slumped, and I saw myself in the mirror of the dressing table, hunched over with the bass saxophone resting the bend of its corpus on the carpet, immersed in a sea of shimmering particles, the unreal light of a grotesque myth, like a genre painting, though certainly no such painting exists: Young Man with Bass Saxophone. Yes, Young Man with Guitar, Young Man with Pipe, Young Man with Jug, yes, young man with anything at all, but not with bass saxophone on worn carpet, young man in golden haze of afternoon sun penetrating muslin curtains, with a mute bass saxophone, the Disney-like rococo of the wardrobe in the background, and the man with his chin sticking up out of the pillow like a corpse. Just a young man with bass saxophone and sleeping man. Absurd. Yet that was the way it was.

I exhaled lightly. A little harder. I felt the reed quiver. I blew into the mouthpiece, running my fingers down the valves; what emerged from the bell like a washbasin was a cruel, beautiful, infinitely sad sound.

Maybe that's the way dying brachiosaurs wailed. The sound filled the beige chamber with a muted desolation. A fuzzy, hybrid tone, an acoustical alloy of some nonexistent bass cello and bass oboe, but more explosive, a nerve-shattering bellow, the voice of a melancholy gorilla; just that one sorrowful tone, sad, like a bell — *traurig wie eine Glocke;* just that one single sound.

It frightened me. I glanced quickly at the man in the bed, but he hadn't moved, the cliff of his chin still jutting out, motionless, like a warning signal. Silence — I suddenly realized that the detached, dangerous voice behind the wall had stopped sputtering — but someone was in the room besides me, the man in the bed, the fly, and the bass saxophone.

I turned around. A haggard little fat man with a flushed bald head and bags under his eyes was standing in the doorway. His eyes were as sad as the tone of the bass saxophone. It was still dying out, fading down the gilded corridors of the hotel, an afternoon wail that must have wakened the guests dozing in their rooms after lunch (officers on leave with their wives, secret couriers on business of the Reich, a homosexual Spaniard who had been living there for the past half year and no one knew why, or what he was doing there, what he was living on, whom he was spying on); it was still fading down the brown dusk of the staircase when a woman's head appeared behind the man's bald pate, gray, curly-haired, two blue eyes, and a big bulbous nose — a clown's face, a living caricature of a woman's face on a bloated woman's body. "Excuse me," I said, but the bald man waved his hands. *"Bitte, bitte,"* he said, walking on into the room, and the woman with the sad face of the clown walked in behind him. She wore high laced boots and an ancient woolen skirt, a Scottish plaid, which glowed drunkenly in the baroque ribbing of the sun's rays in the dust; and behind her came an even more unbelievable figure, almost a midget — no, not almost, he was a midget, he came up to my waist, smaller than the bass saxophone that I was now holding upright, the bend of the corpus resting on the worn carpet (it was only then that I noticed that the carpet bore a woven design of a city emblem, the Czech lion between two towers; someone had tossed a cigar butt on the lion and he was pierced by a black, burned-out hole), but he didn't have the face of a midget; he looked like Caesar: long, thin, tightly closed lips, a Roman nose, a fair lock of hair falling over an intelligent forehead; and it was not a large head on a shrunken body that had had an evil and malicious joke played on it, it was the normal head of a good-looking man on a normal torso — a Caesar cut down to size, I thought; he walked like a duck, and then I noticed that he

really was cut down, from the knees down; he had
no feet, he walked on those knees wrapped in dirty
rags. And like a procession of specters, other apparitions entered the room. A blond, very beautiful girl (at first I wondered whether she didn't just
seem beautiful beside the bulbous nose of the other
woman, but no, later on I saw her from all angles,
her hair falling to her shoulders like broken swan's
wings on either side of a narrow Swedish face with
big gray eyes); she looked at me, at the man in
the bed, at the bass saxophone, she lowered her
eyes, clasped her hands before her, and hung her
head, the fair Swedish hair shading the face which
looked as if it had never been touched by a smile,
as if it had been made of wax, as if she had spent
her whole life somewhere in the darkness of an
air-raid shelter, in the semidarkness of closed rooms
(perhaps she was just a nightchild of Berlin's Moabit prison, where they had made a candle of her
— she shone like Toulouse-Lautrec and burned at
both ends); she stood before me with her hands
locked in front of her, in a dress that merged with
the beige glow, so that all that seemed to be left
was her head — a pair of broken, golden-silver
swan's wings, a countenance the color of alabaster,
ivory, the keyboard of a long-unused piano, and
two gray eyes gazing at the focus of the sunlight
reflecting in the valves of the bass saxophone and
trembling near the lion's paw on the carpet. The

parade was not yet over; behind the girl came a hunchback with black glasses on his nose, and with him a one-eyed giant who led him by the hand. The hunchback groped around with his free hand in the rays of sunlight; he disturbed the fly in its dying; it buzzed, flew around the groping hand a couple of times, and, exhausted, sat down on one of the valves of the bass saxophone, waved its legs desperately, slipped off and tumbled into the huge corpus; the bass saxophone resounded with a terrified buzzing; the hunchback, wearing baggy knickerbockers on his skinny legs, looked like a blind owl. An artificial leg protruded from the giant's trouser leg. The rivets glistened in the sunlight, the semicircle of apparitions stood around me. "Lothar Kinze," declared the gaunt little plump man with the bald head. *Und sein Unterhaltungsorchester,* added the associative instinct within me and silently, against my will, like a panoramic camera my eyes took in the band: the gray woman with the face of a sorrowful clown and a nose like a carnival mask, the cut-down Caesar, the girl with the Swedish hair, the blind hunchback, and the huge man with the artificial leg, who leaned up against the wardrobe with the angels until it creaked, and one angel swayed over and a tiny scale of gold peeled off its curls and fell into the thinning red hair of the man with the artificial leg, champion of the whole world (it seemed to me) in American freestyle wrestling; the fly in the corpus stopped buzzing too — it was late summer, early autumn, the time of death for all flies, and this one had almost outlived its time (but at least it died in a metal horn resembling a temple, with the sounds of the little priest's tiny footsteps — most human beings don't have the privilege of dying that way); silence. It's only a dream, I tried to tell myself, but then I never believed in apparitions, in hallucinations, in scientifically confirmed parapsychological phenomena, I had never believed in anything beyond the borders of the natural, I was an absolute realist, I had never in all my life had any premonitions; when my aunt was dying — she was a beautiful young woman whom I loved with the intimate love of a relative for a hot-house flower of Prague salons (she died at the age of twenty-seven) — I didn't sense a thing, no extrasensory telecommunications, no telepathy; nor did I believe in miracles or in mediums, I laughed at it all, even at the miraculous fellow in the neighboring town who owned a wood-carving shop and had helped the police through a medium, though the town had been full of witnesses; I was a person strictly of this world, and my only myth was music; and so I knew that it was no vision, no apparition, no hallucination, that it was the gang, not the golden gang from Chicago, Eddie Condon and his Chicagoans, but *Lothar Kinze mit seinem Unterhaltungsorchester*. Holy cow, I said to myself, and it was funny all of a sudden, because every deviation from the norm is an impulse to laughter — people are apt to be conventional, and unfeeling toward everything but themselves. But that lasted only a moment; I felt the glance of the girl's gray eyes, the only one of the lot without a stigma, the only one that was not deformed (not physically), and again I didn't believe in telepathy but I had the feeling that she guessed my untoward laughter; an awful feeling, unpleasant to begin with and growing swiftly into an unbearable shame, as if I had been telling a dirty joke at a funeral, relying on the chanted words of the priest to drown out my own and he had suddenly fallen silent, and through the silence, over the dry grass, over the tombstones and the freshly dug earth, the wind had borne some obscene, some unbelievably awkward word instead of a prayer (If Thou wert to weigh iniquity, who would pass?); and that decided it too, that and the bass saxophone that I was still holding in my hand like a bishop holding a bejeweled staff. "Would you like to try it?" asked the man with the flushed bald head and I realized what he reminded me of — monkey with a red face, as if his face had been burned with a flamethrower (it had). He smiled; his smile disclosed his teeth, and again it was no hallucination but reality: it was as if he had been in the hands of some Gestapo man with a perverted sense of humor; half his teeth were missing, but not just the upper or the lower teeth, and not irregularly in either jaw; they were like the keys of a piano, tooth, space, tooth, space, and the upper jaw was the same only inverted (space, tooth, space, tooth) so that when the upper and the lower teeth met they formed an absurd checkerboard (he smiled with his teeth clenched). "Come on," he said. "We'll go down to the stage, and you can try it out there. Doesn't it have a beautiful sound?" "*Ja*," I answered. "Like a bell. Very sad. *Sehr traurig*." "Well, come on," said the man. "Take it along. I'll carry the case."

And so I took the bass saxophone in my arms and walked toward the door. This isn't by force any more, said a cold patriotic voice in my head. So what? I replied rebelliously. A lone *Feldwebel* on the bank of the Ledhuje — and who forced my sister to turn him down? Maybe he could have been the good husband for the short marriage in her life (she never found that marriage, my poor sister, she died of cancer before she turned thirty); at least he wrote poems in a blue notebook, and which one of my sister's local tennis-playing admirers had ever even read a poem? But he probably never came back anyway: it was the winter before Stalingrad; the blue notebook fell into the snow somewhere along the banks of the Volga, and when spring came, and the burned, peeling tanks of Tolbukhin's army chased the Germans through the burned steppe to the west and the last vestiges of the nonsensical, murderous, heroic crew staggered back to the east, the safety zone along the tragic river slowly expanded (and the portentous servants of a new enemy began to rule there), the snow thawed, the blue notebook sank through it to the earth, slipped into the river, the river carried it to the sea, it dissolved there, turned into nothing, all that was left of it was the rhyme that stuck in my head: *in meinem Kopfe kalte Winde wehen,* that echo of Rilke (it's possible that the *Feldwebel* didn't even know it). And so I said "What the heck!" and strode through the brown half-light of the hotel corridor with the bass saxophone in my arms like an overgrown child, on one side of me the man with the checkerboard smile, on the other side the woman with the face of a sorrowful clown, and in front of us once again the old man in the wooden suit, dragging his lame leg crosswise along the runner. As for me, grown up again, I was weaving warp and woof of my defense.

I was eighteen, full of complexes, an unhappy kid, no genius. I only felt, I didn't know; concepts like collective guilt didn't even exist yet. But then, I never believed in anything like that anyway (and my God, how could I have, when I never even believed in individual guilt? How can that square with Christianity? Or with Marxism? For a person

isn't given freedom, but nonfreedom. It would have
been enough if my mother, on one of those excur-
sions to Bad Kudowa, had broken up with my father — they were still only engaged then — and
married the restaurant proprietor who fell in love
with her there and who for a long time after her
wedding, until he himself got married, sent her,
and later even me, gingerbread teddy bears; I
would have been born a German, and since I'm
male, healthy, strong, well-grown, I could easily
have become a member of the SS), I only knew
that on autumn evenings two soldiers used to come
to the Port Arthur bar, and they'd sit in the corner
under the portrait of President Hácha and listen;
we would play Ellington, Basie, Lunceford's arrangements, we would swing as if the devil possessed us, the Port Arthur reverberating like an
immense Victrola into the blacked-out protectorate
night in the town, and we would stare past our
saxophones at those two men in the uniform of the
Nazi Luftwaffe; after the war, a German officer in
occupied Paris named Schulz-Koehn became a
legend — he had concealed an escaped black POW
in his apartment, who along with Charles Delaunay,
in the shadow of the German High Command, put
together *Hot Discography;* but Schulz-Koehn was
not alone — those two soldiers also came out in the
open one day, they pulled some sheet music out
from under their military blouses, Dixieland ar-

rangements of "Liza Likes Nobody" and "Dark-
town Strutters' Ball" (they had picked them up in
Holland in exchange for some arrangements by
Henderson that a band in Athens had allowed them
to copy) and they let us copy them in exchange
for our Ellingtons. Then they disappeared too,
apparently to the eastern steppes: they didn't have
the luck of Schulz-Koehn; but before that they had
been crossing Europe like a pair of missionaries
possessed of a faith without ideology, indeed a faith
which cancels ideologies, like two modern scribes
from some sort of migrant monastery, a monastery
on the march, reproducing secret manuscripts (at
their *Offizierschule* — it seemed incredible, and yet
there's little that seems incredible now after all that
has happened — they had had a band; one of them
was a captain, the other a first lieutenant, and they'd
played Chick Webb, they'd played swing, not for
the public — they had rehearsed Kreuder for the
public — but for themselves, imagine, German ca-
dets in a Nazi *Offizierschule* imitating a hunch-
backed black drummer. So it was not just in
concentration camps, not just in the Jewish town
of Terezín, but in the *Offizierschule* too, it was
simply everywhere, that sweet sickness, it would
have eventually infected everyone, and perhaps if
the war had turned out badly it would have finally
infected the victors, ultimately — even though it
might have taken many years, maybe centuries —

transforming them into people); those two played along with us once, one on piano, the other on drums, and just before they were shipped to the East, they did something awful (everything could, can, be a crime) — Lexa never did explain it so that in the end people spoke badly of him instead of feeling sorry for him (I mean our people, people who called themselves our people): during the reprisals after the Heydrich assassination, the Nazis killed his father, shot him to death, and the day after his name had appeared in the papers ("for approving of the assassination of Deputy *Reichsprotektor* Reinhard Heydrich, the following persons were shot: . . .") those two German officers met Lexa in the town square — where Mr. Káňa had watched me, and where Mr. Vladyka had watched me on another occasion — and a bit awkwardly expressed their sympathy, and shook his hand; he never explained that away (his father not cold in the grave yet and here he goes chitchatting with Germans, in public, just because they listen to his crazy caterwauling); no, Lexa never did live that down.

I walked down the back staircase to the hotel auditorium with the bass saxophone in my arms. The brown twilight was transformed into the murky dusk of dim electric lights. Our procession descended the spiral iron staircase with difficulty. The gray walls of the stairwell formed the background for the procession of shadows that accompanied us, a persiflage of a Disney film, not Lothar Kinze but Snow White and the Seven Dwarfs (the woman with the face of a tragic clown was Sneezy; her incredible nose, a half-pound turnip nose, was multiplied by the shadow to fantastic dimensions. Snow White was equally fantastic in her slenderness and with her two screens of hair, in the shadow picture more hauntingly than ever like the broken wings of a swan, a black shadow swan). And the procession marched on silently, accompanied only by the sounds of disparity, of sickness, of ill-health, the wooden harmony of war: the creaking of artificial limbs and rheumatic joints, the rattle of bronchial passages that had survived a climate to which nature has adapted the metabolism of arctic foxes and penguins, not people. Yet people can bear almost everything, although almost everything leaves its mark on them, almost everything brings them closer to death. We took our beat from the leg of the woodclad old man as it thudded uncontrolled against the stairs, like a tom-tom, and our Turkish drum was the giant's artificial leg. Between the ropes a dark space appeared, within it a bright semicircle frightened out of the darkness of the stage by a dusty cone of light, and in the semicircle around a piano were five music stands, glittering with circus paint and mock jewels forming the big, decorative golden initials LK. *Lothar Kinze mit seinem Unterhaltungsorchester.* We walked out onto the stage, and I stopped with the bass saxophone in my arms directly under the cool spotlight which glared from somewhere overhead in the flies.

They gathered around me. The last to arrive was the cut-down Caesar; the girl with the Swedish hair smiled, and Lothar Kinze, with his flushed pate and checkerboard teeth, looked at me. I realized it was the same look as the old man in the wooden suit had given me in front of the hotel — the look of an unsolved problem. But what problem? Why? What was all this about? The blind hunchback in the swollen knickerbockers raised his white face to the dusty light in the flies; it was a mask of long intimacy with suffering, no longer torture but the permanent pressure of existence deprived of almost all joy, entirely void of all meaning; in the white face the black lenses stared like coal pits; why? What for?

"*Ja,*" I said, and stood the bass saxophone on the plank floor of the stage. The absolute darkness of the stage hung around the cone of light; God knows who could have been watching us from the darkness; a full house (perfectly behaved and silent, and perhaps we were a vaudeville sketch, neither reality nor hallucination, a prehistoric Spike Jones in a humorless world, an exhibit from a live waxworks), or a single spy, Mr. Káňa or his personal agent who would tell all in the broad daylight of Kostelec, except this time Mr. Káňa wouldn't succeed, because Kostelec wouldn't believe this; they honor common sense in Kostelec, not hallucination; they have a saying there, a sort of trademark of the sensible: ". . . in Kostelec. They didn't like it in Kostelec, they don't believe it in Kostelec, they had no patience with it in Kostelec"; with that, you can take care of the opinion of all the world and anybody (I still hear it from the lips of my aunt — on a concert of the Chamber Harmony Ensemble, on an exhibition of abstract painters, on Allen Ginsberg — and even back then the expression was already as old as the hills); it is a town of sensible people; it respects fame, but in all respectfulness tacitly considers its bearers to be nuts, that's to say, somewhat inferior people, even if on a national level they do have a certain useful function to fulfill with respect to Kostelec, the center of the world (adding polish to the concerts of the Kostelec Society for Chamber Music, or symbolizing the cultural level of the state and hence of Kostelec, for the state naturally exists only on account of Kostelec). Here in Kostelec, sensible people do not apply themselves to foolishnesses like Surrealism or inferiority complexes, incomprehensible (comprehensible only to nuts) problems like assonance, the inner organization of a painting as compared to the organization of external reality. Everything exists on account of this

oasis of sensibility, on account of this gilded belly-
button of the world, but above all in order that
Kostelec have something to talk about: actresses'
divorces, poets' scandals, getting drunk in bars —
"it isn't done in Kostelec" — and so I could relax;
even if Mr. Káňa had sent a little spy, *Lothar Kinze*
und sein Unterhaltungsorchester, this baroque,
Brueghelesque detail from the Inferno, was altogether unclassifiable in the categories of Kostelec,
as was the bass saxophone (Auntie: "What good
is an instrument like that anyhow? Bedřich Smetana
has such nice compositions, and he didn't need any
bass saxophone"); and then of course so was I,
in the embrace of Lothar Kinze. But I didn't need
to make any apologies for Lothar Kinze.

What was their problem, then? Lothar Kinze
hurriedly walked up to one of the music stands;
from behind, his clothes hung loosely on him as if
they had been made for someone almost twice as
fat or as if he were a clown whose overcoat is
actually his frockcoat; then he turned to me and
smiled. *"Kommen Sie hier.* Here is the sheet music.
Play." I raised the bass saxophone; it glowed like
a rainbow in the white dusty light; it seemed to
me that they all sighed, as if they had seen something sacred, and then I understood: it too was
blind, etched by time, spittle, verdigris, bad handling, it resembled (in the texture of its metal surface, in its silverwhite, matte texture) an incense

burner that an old rural priest in some atheist country might use for the funeral ritual and which in the yellow light of the poor candles also has that matte glow, that etched sparkle (but because Thou art merciful, abundant is Thy forgiveness). Lothar Kinze handed me the sheet of music. It was the bass saxophone part of a composition originally called "The Bear," *ein Charakterstück für Bassaxophon und Orchester,* but someone's hand had crossed out the title in a faded brown ersatz wartime ink, and had written instead *Der Elefant.* My eyes followed the notes; it was a waltz in A minor, a very simple affair, based on the effect of deep notes, certainly not what I yearned to play on this saxophone — it was no Rollini — although it was exactly what I was capable of playing from sheet music. But again, why?

"You mean, *ein Jam Session?*" I asked. Lothar Kinze looked at me; I could see no comprehension in his eyes; he turned to his orchestra, but they stood in silence, the old man in the wooden suit, with one eye down on his cheek somewhere near the place where his Eustachian tube ended, the woman with the face of a sad clown, yes, the entire catalogue of sadness, of ruins, the giant with the artificial leg, the blind hunchback, the girl with the broken wings of a white swan (our shadows had shrunk to black puddles under our feet), the cut-down Caesar. And he was the one to catch on.

"*Ja,*" he said, "if you wish. But do you read music?" He spoke clearly; his voice was completely intelligent, calm, normal too (all the more pain must have been contained in the soul of that cut-down body that it was complete, not limited by debility or at least a diminished intelligence, nor equipped with the thick skin of a poor memory that must be a property of the souls of achondroplastic midgets). "*Ja,* I can read music." I said. "But I've never played a bass saxophone. The . . . the . . ." The touch, I wanted to say, but my German left me. But Lothar Kinze nodded. I looked again at the bass saxophone, placed the fingers of my left hand on the valves. I sat down, and the Brueghel-esque detail suddenly came oddly to life: Lothar Kinze pulled a violin from out of nowhere (not from out of nowhere, it had been lying on top of the piano), the cut-down Caesar adroitly pulled himself up into a chair and a trumpet glistened in his hands; the giant led the blind hunchback to the vicinity of the drums and the little fellow in the knickerbockers seemed to sense them, seemed to smell the leather skins, his hand reached for the gray cowbells, the expression of painful stress on the white face was replaced by something that was almost happiness; as if he could see, he slipped between the cymbals, and the ballooning knicker-bockers disappeared behind the big drum, flexible nervous fingers found the sticks, and he was ready;

the giant's demistep sounded, he walked over to the far stand where there was a bandoneon and a button accordion, and put it on (we had begun to look down our noses at the accordion. Kamil Bĕhounek played swing on one but we had never heard of a black who did — neither Ellington, nor Lunceford, nor Kirk, nor Basie had an accordion); the big woman with the half-pound nose sat down behind the piano, and on that proboscis of hers she put real pince-nez on a black cord (all the more pre-Spike Jones ur-Spike Jones it became, all the less would anyone believe it; I quit worrying about preparing a defense of my musical collaboration), the ends of which she fastened behind her ear; now she looked as if she had one of those immense papier-mâché party noses with glasses attached, the kind that is held in place by a rubber band around your head; I moistened the reed and they all fell silent again; I gave the instrument a trial blow — the massive painful yell that emerged surprised even me; it spread through the empty auditorium beyond the borders of the light, that labyrinth of wood and plush, of dust and hungry mice and undiscriminating, sated fleas full to bursting with Czech and German blood; yes, the voice of a dying gorilla, a male who had fought and won and had to die. I played a scale, up, down; the tones connected poorly but the touch wasn't too difficult; yet those sobbing ill-breathed inter-tones seemed to have in them something of the character of the Chicago school (perhaps something of that character was also caused by imperfect control of the old, antiquated instruments on the part of the young musicians, who probably wore knee-breeches like the blind drummer). "Good," I said firmly, Lothar Kinze tapped his bow on his violin, placed it under his chin, from his waist up made a rolling, typical waltz motion, the symbol of three-quarter time, and we cut loose. Maybe it was a delusion after all, a vision, an acoustic chimera; if time were made up of transparent cubes like a cosmic set of children's blocks, I would have said that someone had removed a cube from that calm, unsurprising image of Kostelec — some mastermind, some oversoul — and irreverently replaced it with a small transparent aquarium containing Spike Jones's band, for indeed, that's what it was. In the twelve-measure introductory interval I had time enough to observe the *Unterhaltungsorchester* of Lothar Kinze at work in the half-dozen round mirrors on the bass saxophone. Besides, I have ears. The hunchback (he looked as if he were smelling nectar or pork roast with apples or whatever stands for nectar in Bavaria; maybe sweet beer) beat the drum like a machine; perhaps he was wound up with a key, like a completely mechanical drumming apparatus, because he tapped the snare drum with no originality, with no imagination whatsoever, irrevocably, with no gradation, oom-pahpah, oom-pahpah; he didn't move, his bony hands seemed to be attached to the body of a plastic mannequin with an expression of almost optimistic happiness on its frozen face; only the bony hands moved (and the foot in the knicker-bockers' leg on the pedal of the big drum, but I couldn't see it: oom—, oom—), the little hands — pahpah,—pahpah (once, either in a dream or when I was very young, I saw an orchestrion, with a mechanical angel that handled a complete, real percussion system with the same amount of musical intelligence); and under the raised black wing of the piano was the woman with the face of a mournful clown, her nose jerking each measure of the clumsy rhythm of the mechanical waltz forward with a downward and upward movement of her head, the eyes on either side of the carnival-gag nose intently following the fingers of her right, then her left hand; like a third-rate piano teacher in some sub-Alpine Gotham, never a wrong note, never a bit of imagination. To hear such a performance, such a style, is to be stripped of the enchantment of an unrealized and completely foolish dream: a romance of the conservatory, where in twelve practice rooms twelve pianos filling the air with Czerny's *Études* bring to blossom twelve dreams (foolish like all dreams since no one ever remembers that dreams really die when they come true, and reality really isn't a dream), dreams of Steinways, Richter dreams, Van Cliburn dreams; and then the trip (once it had meant hunting for a job, now they allot you a placement slip at school) to one Kostelec or another; and there, first a big success with the local philharmonic or student orchestra, a *Moonlight Sonata* or two, a few *Slavonic Dances,* and then year begins to follow year, and the years consist of months and weeks and lessons every day to four or five little girls from good families (and here and there a little boy from a good family) that have realized the social merits of a musical education: four or five hours a day watching fingers that have trouble hitting the right keys, listening to chords in which there are strange, fantastic tones (when a finger accidentally strikes two keys at once), thirty years of watching and listening; the dream petrifies, as does the flexible movement of the spirit and the nerves and the attractive bare arms of twenty-four-year-olds, the flowing of notes through fingers to brain and ears and back to the keys and the strings which finally pour forth the music, make it live, ring, and sing; all that is left is watching and listening to fingers, the precise mechanical oom-pahpah, oom-pahpah of the left hand and the metallic, impersonal melody of the right, the perfect, depersonalized performance of the perfect idealized pupil, a pupil who in turn will eventually become embodied in the teacher, with thirty years of watching and listening to fingers herself; and

that's the other, less pleasant, more probable out-
come of most dreams: they end up unfulfilled, submerged in the awful rurality of provincial towns
where time slowly extracts the softness from young
bodies and a shell of resignation grows around their
souls, where in the end they conform to Kostelec,
accept its universal position, never again to try for
that one desperate (and vain) recourse of man: to
protest at least, to make provocations at least, if
victory is impossible (and impossible it is, don't let
the poets fool you; it's all just waiting for the
slaughter, the butchery, not the battle). That was
the way she played too, forte, without feeling, with
pedantic accuracy, every bass tone was right, but it
hurt; and the nose pushed each measure ahead,
while in the measures the cut-down Caesar quivered
with an uncontrollable vibrato, with a circuslike
sentimentality, only just on key, and the fierce frown-
ing giant played the accordion so that it sounded
like a barrel organ (heaven knows how he achieved
that sound — he seemed to squeeze the instrument
with immense strength, his big fingers exerting obvious effort to avoid pressing the wrong buttons).
Lothar Kinze played facing the orchestra, in the
white light from the flies I could see the resin pouring off the strings, and as the rolling motion of his
torso disturbed the air, the resin danced off into
the darkness in barely visible, shallow waves; like
the others, he played forte, in supremely senti-

mental chords — all that was missing was an old woman with a harp, and the clink of coins on a courtyard pavement (yet even that was there: the hunchback clinked the triangle); I closed my eyes. It all sounded exactly like a paranoid orchestrion — not only the drums, not only the piano, but the whole unit: Spike-Jonesier than Spike Jones; and then the twelfth measure, and maybe it was the hypnotic effect of the unbelievable mélange of those five dervishes (the girl with the Swedish hair wasn't playing any instrument, and I found out later that she was the singer; the old man in the wooden suit was the errand boy) but when I blew on the saxophone again, it sounded like a caricature too, as if somebody had created a gigantic controllable old automobile horn; I had no trouble with the music, it was ridiculously easy (we were all well-trained on the syncopations in Lunceford's *Sax Tutti*), but I did have trouble with my laughter: a laughing elephant. It really was more like an elephant than a bear (at dinner later, Lothar Kinze told me that the change in the title of the piece was not a result of a re-evaluation of the tonal nature of the instrument, it was an ideological change; it had been renamed after the defeat at Moscow). And still it was a pleasure; soon I forgot to laugh: if you haven't got too much talent and aren't equipped with absolute pitch, playing is always a pleasure, particularly when you're not playing alone — even if it's a piano duet and all the more so in a band. I was playing a bass saxophone for the first time in my life (and for the last — then they disappeared forever, they really no longer exist); it had a touch entirely different from my tenor sax, but as soon as I felt I could make the immense chrome-plated leverwork obey me, could squeeze a melody out of that mammoth hookah, a simple melody but a recognizable one, that the thunderous tone of a contrabass cello would obey the movement of my fingers and the blow of my breath, I was happy. The senseless happiness of music engulfed me like a golden bath; it's a happiness that never depends on the objective, only the subjective, and perhaps it has a more profound link with the humanness of things because it's altogether senseless: the strenuous pro-duction of certain nonsensical sounds — that are no good for anything — for no explicable, reason-able purpose (Auntie: "He was one of those vaga-bonds, a musician, he played in bars and at dances. Even at home he banged on the piano for days on end. In Kostelec no decent person stopped to pass the time of day with him"). And so I played with Lothar Kinze and his *Unterhaltungsorchester,* just as off-key, with just as sentimental a vibrato, a com-ponent of the creaky human orchestrion whose per-formance suggested a loud protest against the waltz, against music in general (it moaned, how dread-fully the orchestra moaned — but that was before

I understood that disharmony, the vibrato trembling almost to derailment), until *Der Elefant* was over. *"Sehr gut!"* cried Lothar Kinze, glancing uncertainly at the woman behind the piano and the girl with the Swedish hair. "And now, if you please," he looked at me, "there's an alto sax on the stand next to you. If you would be so kind . . . we'll try *'Gib mir dein Herz, O Maria!' Bitte."* I reached automatically for the alto, and carefully placed the bass saxophone on the floor. As I was bending down, I again wondered Why? Why this private concert by twilight in an empty theater? Did Lothar Kinze simply have a yen to make music for nothing? And not just he, but the whole ensemble? I postponed worrying about it. We played the tango. Again Lothar Kinze succeeded in giving the whole thing the incomparable sound of a village band, the wailing call that spills out of taverns of a Saturday midnight and together with the murky light pours out over the manure-smelling village green, that insistent throaty weeping and wailing of trumpet and clarinet; my adaptation this time was even more complete, because I knew the alto saxophone better. Only my pleasure was lessened. It was not the bass saxophone, and it didn't drown out the growing mystery. I'm not crazy, I have to ask, I can't just sit here for an hour, for five hours, maybe till morning, adding an alto or bass voice to this squealing disharmonic monstrosity of Lothar Kinze's and then go drown myself in the Ledhuje river in the morning (like my uncle who eluded life in the eleventh grade over an equation; he worked on it all day, all night, my mother thought he was asleep but they found him in the morning, he had hanged himself over the unsolved equation; and there had been no history of suicide in our family, but presumably somebody had to start and to do it in a way that isn't done in Kostelec). So I finally had to ask the question.

"It's been very nice," I said. *"Danke." "Bitte,"* said Lothar Kinze. "Actually, what I wanted . . ." I paused. The problem was staring out of his eyes. The answer to my question. "But now I really have to go." *"Wohin?"* blurted out Lothar Kinze. "Home. They'll be expecting me by now." "Couldn't you phone?" "I guess I could," I said. "I could phone the neighbors." "Do it then. *Bitte.*" There was a plea in Lothar Kinze's voice.

And then I asked, "Why?" and it seemed to me that Lothar Kinze's red bald spot filmed over with sweat. He glanced almost unhappily at the giant with the accordion and then at the cut-down Caesar, but there was no help forthcoming there. The blind man he omitted. He glanced at the girl, at the woman with the nose. She was the one who cleared her throat, turned it (the nose) and the faded eyes at its root around to face me, cleared her throat again and said (in a voice like squeaking shoes): *"Wir brauchen Sie."* We need you.

Either the silence that followed really was funereal or else she gave me such an urgent answer in those three words — not an articulated answer, a deeper one, the one that lies in the intonation (the true meanings of words are always down in the intonation) — that the words expanded in the darkness behind the cone of light. *WIR BRAUCHEN SIE!* Desperately, earnestly, as if she were begging me — and yet she said it softly, without raising her voice, an involuntary SOS of the soul, against which there may be no objection — sadly, urgently; that is the way the voices called from Pandora's box, and when she obeyed and opened it all the ills of the world flew out. *Wir brauchen Sie.* I turned to Lothar Kinze; he was scratching his leg with the violin bow. *"Ja,"* he said, "we need you. For this evening." "But!" I exclaimed, loudly, quickly, because it — nonsense. Nonsense. Here, now, all right. Kostelec won't believe this, a twilight jam session in a side show in an empty theater, but not in the evening. No, not then. In the evening Herr Zeeh will be here, Herr Pellotza-Nikschitsch, heaven only knows what Czech-German ladies, maybe even Mr. Veselý, Wessely the quisling, and maybe even a few of Mr. Káňa's little agents, no, no, no — the

doll shut its eyes, the voice of reason braced itself
for a mighty roar: NO! *"Wir brauchen Sie . . ."*
again, just like the woman with the face of a mournful clown had said it, except this time it was in
another tone, a mezzo-soprano voice in a more attractive, flutelike tone; I looked up. It was the girl
with hair like the broken wings of a swan. "We
need you," she repeated. "If you don't play this
evening, then . . ." and there was that same intonation, that pause so empty that it encompasses the
meaning of entire sentences and long explanations.
And the same desperate plea in her gray, Moabit
eyes. I didn't ask "Why" again. I was seventeen,
eighteen, later on in my life I wasn't as noble,
I pretended not to hear intonations. But this time
I accepted and I didn't question; they had a reason.
Was it connected — I didn't ask, but the association
unfolded inside my head — with the man upstairs
in the beige room, with that unshaven cliff of a chin?
He was undoubtedly the bass saxophone player.
But why the tragic tone? They could play without a
saxophonist. Or else they could postpone the concert. These things happen, after all, particularly
in a war: *vis maior*. God knows what war wound,
what illness knocked that bearded mountain down
onto the beige bed. "But I might be recognized,"
I told Lothar Kinze. "People know me here, and
if they saw me . . ." If it got around that I had

played with a German band, for Germans — but
something stopped my tongue, perhaps it was shame
or perhaps they were the ones that disarmed me,
that they so naturally wanted me to play with them,
Germans, and it must have been more dangerous
for them than for me, contact with a lower race —
or was it only sexual contact that was meant? Certainly that, at any rate. (No, no danger. Whole
crowds of Czechs played in German bands — Chrpa,
the trombone player, he died there.) But the fact
that they asked me, that the old dame from the
Bavarian hills put it in the form of a plea, We need
you! that they didn't force me, that they didn't
simply order me — it would have shamed me to
say that I was afraid to play with a German band
because I was known there, something as natural
as that (but what is natural, after all? Would anybody have thought, in the years of that war, when
concentration camps were tolerantly devouring
Jewish industrialists and Communists, pot-bellied
functionaries of the patriotic Sokol physical culture
organization along with consumptive weavers from
the Mautner mill, and when people lowered their
voices because *Der Feind hört mit* — the Enemy is
listening — and a joke could mean the firing squad,
would anyone have thought that only a few years
would pass and pot-bellied Sokol functionaries and
Jewish industrialists would be wielding picks and

shovels again, this time mining uranium, although there would be no *Feind*, no Enemy in the land; what in the world is natural, what is certain, absolute?), so I didn't finish my sentence. Lothar Kinze might even have been uninformed, perhaps he had been traveling with his grotesque band through the Old Reich, and this was his first performance in a Protectorate of the Third Reich because he said, "By whom don't you want to be recognized?" "By Herr Kühl." I said the first, most dangerous name to pop into my head. "He has no liking for me."

I needn't have added that. They exchanged glances again, and the woman behind the piano cleared her throat. Horst Hermann Kühl: the name mentally slotted itself into place too, and along with it sounded the mad, threatening voice behind the wallpaper. Was that why? But if so, why? "We could," said the woman with the face of a mournful clown, clearing her throat, "we could disguise you somehow." "*Ja,*" said Lothar Kinze, "we could, we have the things to do it with." He looked at me. "If you are willing . . ." A pause, and in it the anxiety of a problem that must be solved, or else. "Please," came the voice from Moabit, "please, we truly need you," said the girl with the Swedish hair. I looked around. They were all looking at me — even the blind man's dark glasses mirrored the saxophone that I was still holding in my hand. In the corpus of the bass saxophone on the floor, the dying fly gave a last sob. I could smell the old, weak, desperate smell of resin in my nose.

"All right," I said. "I'll go and make a phone call."

I thought up some excuse or other on the phone. Then I came back. In an hour we had worked through Lothar Kinze's entire repertoire: a miserable medley of waltzes, tangos, and foxtrots, indiscernible from polkas or schottisches or any composition with an even number of beats per measure; no problems; it was extraordinary (or perhaps it was part of the chimera, of the *Fata Morgana*) that this bundle of worn-out hackneyed songs, melodies played and replayed so often that you no longer perceive them, harmonies as similar one to another as one cliché is to another, extraordinary that this set of songs, like their style without a single bit of originality or inspiration, without imagination, was Lothar Kinze's stock-in-trade for (judging by the stickers on the accordion case) almost all Europe; perhaps they used to travel with a hard-luck circus that finally burned down one day somewhere near the front line or after a partisan attack, or else the one and only lion ate up the one and only dancing bear or the one and only bareback rider and there was nothing left to show even the most grateful and undemanding wartime audience; and so they gained their independence, except for the inherited repertoire (there was even *Die schöne Zigeunerin*, "Oh, play to me gypsy . . ." and a sad, beautiful hit from the time when my mother was young: "I'm forever blowing bubbles, Pretty bubbles in the air. They fly so high, Almost to the sky" — our band used to play it too, but in swing), and they traveled from town to town, through villages, along the side-lines of the war, cheering up the German com-munities in distant and peripheral countries of the occupation; perhaps it was also a form of beggary, maybe the band really did belong in courtyards, but the German communities had at their disposal the best art nouveau halls in all Serbian, Polish, Macedonian, and Ukrainian towns, just like ours in Kostelec (with lunettes from the original design by Master Mikoláš Aleš), and so the ensemble of Lothar Kinze also had at its disposal the best halls in town theaters; from the patched tent of some flop of a wartime circus to the gilded splendor of twisted iron balustrades and plump alabaster breasts of caryatids that looked as if Mucha had painted them — that was the good fortune of all that was fourth-rate in the Third Reich and in all other fourth-rate empires. The girl didn't sing, we did not have time for that. I was only proving that I could handle it; so after an hour we sat down in a room of the hotel (not the room where the bass saxophone player was lying chin up, another one) to eat supper. They brought it up from the hotel kitchen in a big, beaten-up stoneware dish — it was a sort of *Ein-topf,* turnip ambrosia; everyone got a spoon and so did I, we piled it on plates, we ate; it was a supper like Lothar Kinze's repertoire, but they ate humbly, silently, very modestly; a kind of ritual: I could almost see the interior of some circus trailer, the dirty hands of some skinny cook; for that matter, the room itself might have been a circus trailer, the wallpaper striped pink and baby blue (broad, art nouveau stripes and on the stripes, faded gold butterflies — the entire hotel was like a zoo from the mad dream of an infantile paper hanger), the furniture made of square brass bars, with faded silk cushioning between the bars at the head and foot of the bed. We were sitting around a marble table on brass legs which they had dragged to the middle of the room. "What about the man next door?" I asked Lothar Kinze. "Is he your saxophone player?" *"Ja,"* nodded Lothar Kinze, his hand shaking. A piece of turnip stew fell back into his plate, made a splashing noise, and Kinze did not finish his sentence. "Isn't that pretty?" said the woman with the big nose. She nodded out of the window, and cleared her throat. Through the round window, Kostelec offered Lothar Kinze and his orchestra a view of its square. It was almost seven o'clock in the evening and a cheerful procession of workers involuntarily transferred to the Messer-schmitt airplane factory were going past, on their way from the factory after a twelve-hour shift; but that wasn't what was beautiful — what she meant was the church, golden pink, old Gothic, spread out on the square, broader than it was high, settled into breadth like a stone pudding by almost ten centuries of existence, with the wooden shapes of two pudgy moss-covered towers shining green as a forest meadow and above them two red-painted belfries, like two chapels of Our Lady on two green meadow-covered hills, all this rooted in the drop of honey that was the town square, surrounded by lava in the honey and raspberry evening. "Like where I come from in Spiessgürtelheide," sighed the woman. *"Mein Vater"* — she turned to her companions who were silently transferring turnips from plate to mouth — "My father had a butcher shop there, and sausages, a beautiful store on the square." She sighed. "It was all pale green tiles, *ja ja, das war vor dem Krieg,* before the war, a long time ago. I was a young girl then." She sighed.

"And we had the very same church there," she said, pointing at the pudgy towers that looked like colored ice cream ornaments on a well-settled pudding. "At my confirmation, we stood around the church," she related, looking at me fixedly from both sides of that surprising nose. "We had beautiful dresses, silk, white, *ja,* all white," she said, "each of us had a prayer book in her hand and a wax candle with a green wreath, and his Excellency

Bishop Stroffenski went from one to the next, giving us the Holy Sacrament. And he gave each of us a holy picture, oh, it was so wonderful. Each of us put her picture in her prayer book. People had much more respect for holy pictures then, my dear departed mama had a couple of hundred, from all over Europe. Even from Lourdes. *Ja, ja,*" she said. "Bishop Stroffenski was a lovely man, so big and fat, his chasuble was all ironed, as if he had been born into it, not a single fold, not a wrinkle. Everything brand new. That was before the war. *Ja.* And as he went from one to the next he prayed in such a beautiful voice in Latin, and gave out those holy pictures, and out from behind where all of us little girls were standing came my father with two apprentices and Mother, the apprentices carrying a big pot full of hot sausages and Mother a loaf of bread and a knife, and behind her came a third apprentice with a basket full ot bread, and every time the Bishop said a prayer and made a benediction and gave another holy picture, the girl crossed herself and turned to my father and he pulled a pair of hot sausages out of the pot with a hook he had, and Mother cut a slice of bread from the loaf, and the girl got her refreshments there and then. *Ja, Ja.* That's how it was before the war. All that's over with."

Industrialist Řivnáč's shiny car drove past across the square, and the woman saddened. "*Ja,*" said the cut-down Caesar, "before the war. I used to play chess. That's all I was interested in, just chess. All I did was solve problems. Check and mate in the third move, Indian system and so on. I remember all the times we played all day and all night, we didn't even go to school sometimes, we risked everything for a game of chess. I wasn't even interested in girls. Weren't *they* interested though. Take Ursula Brumney, for instance. The town apothecary's daughter. But I was blind, only chess, nothing but chess. And so one day she got an idea. Female. She got herself a checkered dress, it looked like a chessboard. She had to go all the way to Munich to get that material, she told me about it later. Chessboard after chessboard, one next to the other, with printed chessmen, a different problem on each of them. It was only then that I began to be interested in her. But that was the way I was. We were sitting out beyond the town in a beautiful meadow, it smelled pretty as if somebody had spilled perfume on it, but it was only hay, and with a moon in the sky like that clock on the church tower but without the face, yellow as a cat's eye, and we weren't even talking, we were whispering, she was all feverish, I put my arms around her, she lay back in the hay, and then that damned dress, the moon shone on it and I saw the problem on her skirt, a strange problem, a difficult one, and that was the end of that."

The cut-down Caesar laughed. "All I could see was that problem. I thought I'd be done with it in a hurry — what could you expect from some textile designer? — but it was probably copied from some grand master's book or something. Well, I thought I'd solve the problem on the spot and then finish the work of love. *Ja,* but the thing took me two months, two months with almost no sleep at all and not going to work at all until I mated black in the seventh move." "And Ursula?" asked the girl with the Swedish hair. "Her?" said the cut-down Caesar. "She married a master locksmith. Now he's a political leader in Oberzweikirchen." The girl bent her head. The door of Mr. Řivnáč's limousine opened and out stepped his daughter Blanka into Mr. Lewit's house; she was going to her ballet lessons, her slippers hung over her shoulder by their satin ribbons. The limousine started off again.

"*Ja, ja,*" said the giant with the artificial leg, "before the war, I used to drink beer. And how! I was the champion of Schwaben. And it was a woman that kept me from winning the title of champion of Hessen," he declared, "that time we were drinking in Lutze's brewery, me against Meyer from Hessen. He had fifty double steins in him already, and me, forty-nine, he gave up at the fifty-first, he couldn't keep it down any more, he threw it up. And me, I took a double stein and tossed it down as if it was my first that night. But what happened! It stayed in my gullet, a column of beer in my gullet, you see? From my stomach up my gullet to my mouth. I was all full of beer. I had to lean back so it wouldn't spill out, and I felt I couldn't keep it down for long. But we had a rule, whatever goes over the threshold counts as drunk. So I got up and walked over to the door. Slow and easy, my head back so it wouldn't spill out, and I was at the door, almost over the threshold, and then — where the devil don't dare, he sends a woman. Lotti, old Lutze's daughter, a giggling kid, bounces through the door with an armload of double steins, not looking where she's going, bumps into me, and I tell you the beer came squirting out of me like an Iceland geyser. I didn't keep it down over the threshold, so I didn't beat that Meyer fellow who was champion of Hessen." The man with the artificial leg sighed. "*Ja*, that's how it was before the war," he added, and began to stuff himself with the turnip stew.

One after another they emerged from dream into the reality of speech, of anecdotes. They were no longer a vision, a fantasy, it was rather the sticky-sweet panorama of the town square that was unreal, that honey-sweet canvas with the pink-yellow church like a settled pudding, the beautiful Blanka, almost as lovely as the princess of the aquariums (all those rich girls were beautiful as far as I was concerned; I admired rich people, they had rooms paneled with wood, fragrant cigars, all the booty of that luxurious past of our mass-produced times, lives less like life than a dream). I closed my eyes, I opened them. They were still there: the half-pound carnival gag, now without the pince-nez, the intelligent countenance of the cut-down Caesar, the wooden old man with the burnt-out eye in the middle of his cheek, the white face of the hunchback which had lost its expression of happiness and now reflected again the ceaseless pain of existence, Lothar Kinze, red as a baboon's bottom, absent-minded, nervous. But the shining picture of the colorful square and the sunny evening had fallen over them, and it was no longer a funeral march down an iron staircase; and the Swedish girl with the broken swan's wings said, "And I told him, if you kiss me, I'll leave," her silver-gold head against the pink-and-blue striped background like the head of a preclassical Greek statuette: golden hair, ivory complexion, opal eyes, "and so he never kissed me. He was a mathematician. He didn't have the slightest bit of a sense of humor, a sense of playing the game, a sense for foolishness. Well, it wasn't really a matter of a sense of humor, but rather of the game, girls have to talk like that, after all, they can't just say, 'Come with me, boy, I like you! Kiss me! Come to me! Put your arms around me!' and so on." The first smile appeared between the broken wings, but it was a sad, sad smile.

"Usually, the girl has to say No, if you do so and so, I'll go away. But all he knew were the laws of mathematics, not the rules of the game, the little foolishnesses. I said No and he didn't understand. And so nothing came of it. Later," she grimaced (yes, that's right, that's just what she did, she grimaced), "I stopped saying No on account of him. And that was a mistake too." "To him?" asked the hunchback. "No, to others of course," answered the girl. "And what became of him?" asked the blind man. "Don't know," she said. "He's probably a soldier now." "He may well be," said the blind man. "That is unless he . . ." He didn't finish his sentence. "But for that he needn't be a soldier," he added.

And once again they fell back into the dream, like stones into a mosaic. The pumpkin stew (or the turnip stew or whatever it was, the *Eintopf*) in the dish was disappearing. The older woman leaned over the bed, pulled out a suitcase, opened it; a pile of objects wrapped in paper appeared. She placed two on the table. One was a small loaf of black bread, the other was something yellow in a white container. She opened it. "Dessert," she said. The girl cut the loaf into eight slices, the woman spread the yellow stuff on the bread. It melted sweet and bitterish on the tongue, and it burned a little. "*Ach*, honey," said Lothar Kinze. "When I was a little boy, before the war," he said, and I suddenly realized what it was — synthetic honey, ersatz honey, a horrible mess produced by German industry, we had it at home too, once in a while. "The Count had three hundred beehives," Lothar Kinze went on dreamily, "three hundred hives. Hundreds of thousands of bees. Oh, and in the spring, when they were flying home from the fields, their full little behinds smelled so sweetly that all Bienenweide smelled of honey. And the Count!" He waved a hand, a piece of ersatz honey fell in the turnip bowl. But he didn't notice it. "Such a good man! And the Countess! People like that don't exist nowadays. Every year on the Countess's birthday we used to go to congratulate her, all the children from the entire Bienenweide estates. There were so many children, four maybe five hundred or more. We stood in a line down the corridors, down the castle stairs, through the park to the park gate and sometimes even farther. But we weren't bored. The Count had the castle band come and march from the castle gate to the park gate and back, playing for us children. *Ja, uns Kindern.* And when our turn came we walked into the Countess's parlor, she sat in an armchair by the window and she was beautiful, oh how beautiful she was. Women just aren't that beautiful any more. And we each of us kissed her hand, and she smiled at each of us, and with her other hand she reached inside a bundle that she had ready there and gave each child an

imperial ducat. They were good people, *ja, ja*,"
said Lothar Kinze, "before the war. No, sir. There
just aren't any good people like that any more.
And in the evening, they had fireworks in the park,
and the bells in the village rang out." As if in reply,
Gabriel and Michael in their little red belfry
chapels across the street began to peal. "Seven
o'clock," Lothar Kinze came back to earth. "We are
going to have to start getting — " He looked at me.
"And you — if you're sure — we'll have to disguise you a little, won't we?"

"*Ja*," I said quickly. "Absolutely."

And now into another room, a third room, in the
hotel. It belonged to Lothar Kinze, little red spiders
clambered over pea-green wallpaper. And there in
a dirty mirror I was transformed into one of them.
Lothar Kinze pulled a box of makeup out of a suitcase (I had guessed right, they must have recently
been traveling with a circus, there was a collection
of clown's noses, bald wigs with a wreath of red
curls, and all sorts of beards) ; he pasted a big black
mustache under my nose, a mustache that curled
up at the ends, and big black eyebrows. I looked a
little like Groucho Marx, unrecognizable (not like
the time I was sitting in for sax player Heřmánek,
the barber, at the Slavia night club, and they pasted
a Gable mustache under my nose; everybody recognized me and the next evening I didn't play there),
a fitting part of the Spike Jones picture. And then

back to the first hotel room: the chin still jutting up
from the pillow, still the same weak, rattling breathing. But it was beginning to get dark, a green
shadow fell over the room (a reflection from the
moss on the church towers). I took off my jacket,
hung it over a chair. From the closet, Lothar Kinze
handed me the bass saxophone player's uniform:
yes, it fitted the picture. Kelly-green jacket with
purple satin facings, a white shirt and an orange
bow tie. When we came out into the hall, the others
were there waiting, the hunchback and the one-
legged giant clad in the same splendor, looking like
colorful chewing-gum wrappers (obviously a fourth-
rate one-ring side show of a circus). The girl had a
dress of dark purple brocade, closely fitted to her
body (she really was beautiful, and not just in
comparison with Lothar Kinze's mandragoras); by
then I knew whom she reminded me of: Mitzi, the
beautiful prostitute from the Castle House, whom
I loved (I was seventeen, eighteen) as much as I
loved Domanín's daughter (but for different reasons, the opposite feelings, other associations); the
only way we ever saw Mitzi was when she hurried
across the promenade, pale, platinum blond, im-
mensely pretty and attractive, and then one day
Ulrych and I set out to see her, we saved up for it
out of our allowances; but in the lobby of the Castle
House (it was very gloomy, not the least bit luxurious) we got cold feet and we cut out, we only

glimpsed her at her door, in a negligee with a plunging neckline (we spent the money saved for that beautiful prostitute getting drunk on cheap taproom liquor; they had to call a doctor for Ulrych). And after that we only saw her occasionally in the afternoons, in the street, for a brief moment; she was the property of her myth — under her thick fair mane, in a tight skirt with the lovely lines of her behind curving under it, on terribly sad beautiful legs, as unapproachable and as mysterious, but differently, as Blanka Řivnáč, who also occasionally crossed town proudly (on foot!) in her chinchilla coat, smelling of gasoline: a myth too of the town, of the promenade, of the street. When the war was over, a textile worker married Mitzi, and later, for some political or black-market reason, they locked them both up in jail. After that she was a blotchy old woman, but for that matter even the myth of the town disappeared, the myth of the promenade, there was no promenade any more, everything disappears, becomes extinct, fades, dies. Lothar Kinze joined us in the same Kelly-green and purple uniform, and for the second time that day we started the march to the depths of the hotel. No sooner had we left the section where there was natural lighting than shadows began to flicker on the walls; we were Snow White and the Seven Dwarfs again, except I was one of them now. And again the wooden harmony of war. They had dropped the curtain on the stage. The somber (now lighted) space of the auditorium was separated from us by a wall of velvet, and we sat down in a semicircle behind the music stands.

I walked over to the curtain. That stage had been hallowed by the names of splendid bands of days past. Emil Ludvík, Elite Club, Karel Vlach. They used to pull a black backdrop up behind them, and behind it, leaning against a pile of auxiliary curtains and backdrops I used to crouch and listen to that heavenly music; and I heard Milada Pilátová, Gypsy — they called her Gypsy — and from behind the backdrop I overheard them talking during the intermission, and saw her through a hole too. Later, they were said to have run her out of Zlín for drunkenness and prostitution: the young women from the Bata factories led her out of the Grand Hotel in Zlín; that's the way it always is, they always arouse so much hatred, they are always thrown out, run out, prohibited, perhaps they hit too close to the soul, and the ones that don't have any soul can't stand that language, that testimony, that Idea in the cavities where their soul ought to be; but before it happened, she sang (for about three weeks; great historical epochs have often been very short, but their greatness is remembered, and in legend they seem to expand) in the clubs on Zlín's Basin Street, between the Grand Hotel and the movie house, where from behind the blackout curtains in the windows of coffee houses and wine shops the glimmering riffs carried through the wartime protectorate night; Gustav Vicherek and his band (all of them in white jackets, shoulders like moving men, Django Reinhardt mustaches, the light swinging syncopation of strings through the amplifier) and across the street Honza Číž — like the erstwhile duels of bands in old New Orleans, quite friendly — and down the street a-ways Bobek Bryen with Inka Zemánková, whose coarse voice woke Bata's young men from their sleep and drove them en masse to the cold showers; everything — the wartime night, the lights glimmering through the blackout curtains, young people who made the difficult wartime hitch-hiking trek all the way from Prague simply for the music, the dressed-up protectorate movie-makers, students in knee-breeches with hungry eyes swallowing breaks like the word of the Lord, soldiers who wanted to forget the glory of death, night owls, sheep, burnt-out candles — everything was swinging and diving on that Perdido Street of our imagination from the Grand Hotel to the movie house, on that tin-pan alley, swinging and diving in the semiprohibited Milneburg joys of the wartime renaissance of swing, and Gypsy was Queen of Jazz here, the briefest but most dazzling reign in the history of monarchies, the mythical era of Gypsy. Then they locked Vicherek up for "the public performance of eccentric Negroid music," the coffee houses fell silent, Honza Číž took off on tour and died in an icy ditch, Inka Zemánková began vegetating in the Vltava Café, the cold winds of police intervention blew down Perdido Street; now it's nothing but a legend, too; you can't distinguish between what happened and what is a dream; so swiftly gone; but that is the way it should be. I stood there at the curtain, a glass-covered peephole glittered and I put my eye to it; I was overcome with sadness. Honza Číž was already dead, Gypsy had disappeared somewhere in Brno. Fritz Weiss was in Terezín, that concentration camp of a ghetto. I was an adult, I ought to have been taking up serious things and not foolishness. Somewhere, everywhere, little groups like us (I mean us, not Lothar Kinze) played that sad, beautiful music called swing, also doomed to extinction. I looked through the peephole. Right in front of me sat Frau Pellotza-Nikschitsch with a diamond necklace around her neck (or something that looked like a diamond necklace, although that's probably exactly what it was: I think it used to belong to Mrs. Kollitschoner, just like the Pellotza-Nikschitsches' apartment), dressed in red silk. Herr Pellotza-Nikschitsch sat beside her, in the brown shirt of the SA, grim-faced, with a crew cut. Now a German, before that an Italian, before that a Serbian, before that, heaven knows what. Almost impressive in all these metamorphoses; how did he actually feel and what actually was he? His son was a drunk and a brute. He came to a violent end. And next to him Herr Zeeh, also in uniform, black this time, maybe SS or NSDAP or OT or another of those cold abbreviations, an earnest shop assistant in Benno's grandfather's shop, now an earnest member of the Party, and his wife, with a big antique gold brooch, a brooch that I had also seen somewhere else (I had the feeling, I was almost sure), on the dress of someone presumably dead by now (all of it was stolen; the splendor based on exploitation was transformed into a splendor of simple robbery and murder). A velvet gown; and behind it other satined and brocaded German ladies with a mobile jewelry exhibition, the origin of which could not have been reliably proven in a more strictly legalistic society, little shining stories ending in death; and black, brown, and gray uniforms; a panorama of iron crosses. They gathered here as on a painting by the modern Hieronymus Bosch, arranged in a gray-brown impression, to listen to *Lothar Kinze mit seinem Unterhaltungsorchester.*

I was suddenly obsessed with the mad feeling that this was all a trick, that afterward that crowd of gentlemen in boots like leather mirrors would take Lothar Kinze, smear him with tar and cover him with feathers, tie him to a post and then with a vengeful roar carry him past the Nazi Party secretariat to the Ledhuje river. I turned around. Lothar

Kinze stood there in the green and purple jacket, his red pate in the cool light of the spot like a cock-eyed strawberry forgotten in a wine glass of opalescent crystal. He was leaning against the piano, silent. Behind him, over the much-fingered keyboard of the piano, the face of the woman who looked like a sad clown; she had on a black dress with green lace at its neck; the pince-nez were already in place at the root of the indescribable schnozzola; and the hunchback, the cut-down Caesar, and the giant, shiny, purple, and Kelly-green, were immersed in gloomy silence; they were waiting, once again, humbly; something of the humility of the evening was also in what was expected of the performance — the sad funeral gang back from a long journey somewhere in Europe, possible only in wartime, dragging its weepy and incomprehensible message from the glories of one ornate municipal hall to the next, in distant towns on the periphery of big battlefields; the blind man's face was still twisted in an expression of suffering; the golden girl in purple brocade was sitting on a chair next to the piano with her head bent; behind the scenes the Czech stage manager, who knew me (but who hadn't recognized me, at least I hoped he hadn't), was standing ready at the control panel with switches and rheostats; he too was gloomy, but because he had to serve the Germans. I looked through the peephole again. Another side show:

Horst Hermann Kühl had just arrived, gaunt, an unbelievably perfect German in the black uniform of the SS, and the concert could begin.

I hurried back to my chair. Lothar Kinze made a signal with his head, perhaps it was meant as encouragement, picked up his bow, applied the resin to it spiritedly. Another microscopic storm broke over the stage. The bass saxophone was no longer on the floor beside me; it was in a stand that somebody (apparently the wooden old man) had set up, and now it resembled the beautiful neck of a silvery water monster. The woman with the face of a mournful clown was ready, her hands on the keys, every finger on the right key of the introductory chord, her faded little eyes fixed on Lothar Kinze. The sticks in the bony hands of the blind hunchback rested lightly on the skin of the snare drum. The cut-down Caesar moistened his lips, the giant held his little bandoneon. We were waiting, like the Philharmonic at Carnegie Hall under the baton of a purple Toscanini with a pate like a baboon's bottom.

The rustling in front of the curtain quieted down. Lothar Kinze raised his hand with the bow, the girl with the hair like a swan's broken wings got up and walked over to the microphone. There was a rattle and a flurry, the curtain separated at the middle, and an expanding slit of dark hall glared back at us; the stage manager turned up all the

spots. Lothar Kinze tapped the belly of his violin
four times and lit into the strings: its sad voice
clambered up to a touching height; I joined in on
the alto sax; to my left the bandoneon wept and
the trumpet with its dull mute sobbed. And the girl,
with no introduction, with no theme (or was that a
theme?) started in: her voice surprised me; it
sounded like a burst bell, a deep alto, so sad, I
thought, like a bell.

> *Kreischend ziehen die Geier Kreise.*
> *Die riesigen Städte stehen leer. . . .*

We took that beautiful voice of hers (it must
have been beautiful once, before the war; so the
times and their evil powers had even destroyed
something in her; it was a cracked, broken, tattered
voice, a hoarse voice, it wasn't until years later that
something similar came into style but then the
fashion was sweet singing, soprano, like grand
opera, very dignified; there is often humor in a
hoarse voice, but not there: only the sadness of a
burst bell, of strings that are no longer flexible; a
beautiful, once-dark and resounding alto as full of
static as an old gramophone record, night over a
burned forest, no longer the rustle of dried branches
but the creaking, the charcoal crackling of skeleton
trees all over the immense plain of Europe sick
and razed with fire and boils wherever Lothar
Kinze jounced his little gray bus, along paths bor-

dered by columns of smoke touching the sky like huge poplars) and we surrounded her voice with that medley — this time mezzoforte — with the immobile creaky pulse of derision, with a shameless brassiness; and in the middle of it all, one half of her voice, the alto half, was in tune while the other half, flageolets of her scarred vocal chords, joined our distonal catcalling — like rolling voices in a synagogue, each complaining for itself yet, in a choir of many voices, complaining about a common fate, incapable of common song, only of separate, merging, disharmonically complementary off-key chants: the loud mechanical rhythm of the woman with the huge nose, the voices of trumpet and bandoneon (in unison in the arrangement but slightly out of tune, which lent their whine a flavor of piano blues) and even my saccharine voice, with Lothar Kinze trying desperately to add some embellishment; that same odd contrast, beauty and ugliness, the girl's looks and ours, the beauty of half that deep and absolutely musical alto voice and the picturesque brass of the six clowns' circus sentimentality:

> *Die Menschheit liegt in den Kordilleren,*
> *Das weiss da aber keiner mehr. . . .*

And before me, on the waves of distonality, the world of Horst Hermann Kühl, his discipline, and his fertile German women bloated by the loud sentimentality of garden restaurants in Berlin Pankow, melted in that weepy abandonment like the Führer's bust made of chocolate (in the neighboring town, a Sudeten-German town, master baker Düsele, whose shop was on the town square, had made the bust to celebrate the day that the Sudeten region was annexed by the Reich — the skin of almond paste, the mustache and hair of dark chocolate, it was a faithful image of the Führer; but Düsele's display window faced south, and the day of annexation was welcomed by the sun; the swastika symbols hanging all over town did not cast enough shade. Shortly after lunch, the Führer began to collapse, the sugar white of one eye came loose and slowly slid down the melting almond cheek until it fell to the floor of the display window, among the sour candy sticks with red roses through their centers, among the lollipops and chewy penny-crocodiles. About two o'clock in the afternoon the Führer's nose started to get longer and longer, then it melted and his whole face began to stretch; it acquired a bitter, supernaturally sad expression, chocolate tears began to flow down his cheeks like drops of wax from a black sabbath candle and by evening the pastrymaker's beautiful sculpture had been transformed to an approximation of its shape, to a horrible, chewed-up, sad outline, a protean putrefying corpse of a head; in the cool of the evening it hardened, and when the master baker

returned from the garden party on that glorious day
of annexation he was met by the Gestapo, and the
display window was chastely painted over. What
they did with the bust I don't know, perhaps they
destroyed it, or ate it, or maybe the master baker's
successor made almond-paste pigs out of it — such
is sometimes the fate of statesmen) ; song after song,
and the strict countenance of that Teutonic tribal
chief on enemy territory, Horst Hermann Kühl,
softened into a crooked distant smile, a blissful
dream that was reflected on the faces of the German
women around him; Lothar Kinze, a water goblin
in purple satin, leaned with immense sadistic energy into his muddy chords; the giant held on to the
bandoneon like the proverbial child to its mother's
apron, and the cut-down Caesar, as though in love
with the mute, kept up with the accordion player.
But the more horrible it all was and the more it
seemed to me that a rotten egg or apple core must
soon come flying out from behind the iron crosses
and the full maternal bosoms in the first row, the
more real was the dream that settled in Kühl's eyes;
the shell of self-assurance slipped away, the typical
stance of conquerors who are great, brutal, master-
ful men everywhere but at home, that almost inso-
lent, imperious *Romanus sum;* it slipped away, and
our ramshackle expression of bliss became the backdrop for a tiny, weary craving for some Bavarian or
Prussian town, for *Lederhosen,* for the warm world

of an insignificant home where he wouldn't have to
live in a five-room suite in an apartment house on
the main street, with the Führer on an altar, but
where he could be the way he was before the order
of ruthlessness and German greatness, an order that
he had embraced on a money-grubbing impulse or
perhaps merely out of stupidity; the distonal harmony, the cracked voice, the illegible, precise but
deadened basses of the piano — the more dreadful
it all was, the sweeter it sounded to the ear of his
soul (or whatever it was he possessed) and in the
ears of those plump German marketwomen and
public servants who had made their fortunes from
petty assortments of villainy transported here to
this gilded art nouveau hall from marketplaces and
guard booths by an idea born in a beer hall. The
Kostelec String Quartet used to play here in better
days — two professors from the classical lyceum,
the head surgeon from the hospital, and the book-
seller; and then there was the Czech Nonet, the
Philharmonic, that held subscription concerts for
the local islands of culture and civilization and for
local snobs; now the concert was for this assembly
in stolen diamonds and it was *Lothar Kinze mit
seinem Unterhaltungsorchester* that was playing.

And once an orchid had flowered here (when
they raised the curtain, it was as if a blue rose of
new realization had blossomed on the light-flooded
stage): the R. A. Dvorský jazz band; who knows,

I thought, it's one of those funny things: the band with only a few drops of jazz . . . heaven knows what the rest was, but then each of us gets trapped on his own absurd flypaper — something that his particular Kostelec, even those broader Kostelecs of our world, will never understand: it is that treacherous moment when the gate to life appears to open, yet onto a life that is unfortunately outside this world and outside the things praised by this world — not the gate to art, but to sensation, to euphoria, perhaps to an optical, acoustical illusion but certainly the gate to that being's essence, that creature who is childish, naïve, superficial, lacking profundity or exalted emotion, primitive, helpless, like being human is being helpless, who may even be ignorant of the magic word that opens the gate to a better life; but that moment is what determines one's life, once and for all; the diamond of that experience (maybe a glass one, but not a stolen one) is set into the memory: how the curtain went up, how the fortissimo of the brasses shook the hall in syncopated rhythm, how the saxophones blazed honey-sweet, and the decision was made, for a lifetime; the old, mythical illusion of something that will ultimately destroy us, because it is the anchor of youth, the bond to infantilism, because it becomes an illusion that lasts too long, and you can't start all over again then, by then it may be too late for everything. I played; the strength of that musical weakness squeezed me into the ridiculous ranks of Kinze's show; I wailed like a musical clown on a borrowed alto sax, tears ran down my cheeks, I didn't know why, one never knows — sorrow perhaps that one has to die just when one is beginning, that age-old Alpha-Omega. I didn't even see Horst Hermann Kühl; Lothar Kinze's purple back wheeled in front of me, bordered by the wildly flying, wildly fallible bow of his violin, the girl from Moabit sang in a cracked voice, *Es geht alles vorüber, Es geht alles vorbei.* Like a rolling ship in a trough of time, like a wedge of feverish delirium inserted between a normal afternoon that had ended beside a gray bus and a night that undoubtedly would be normal too (I didn't believe in supernatural phenomena) on a bed, under a window with a starry sky, no, Kostelec would not believe this — and suddenly I saw myself among those specters, how terrible it all was; a sharp, pointed, cruel instant of realization: how I had been led into this stuffy, inhuman failure of a world, a soft baby woven of a dream; how the dream kept breaking through, but not a grandiose dream at all, a pathological dream of helplessness and incapacity, marked by illness, girls' derisive, pointed laughter, lack of talent, lonely afternoons at the movies, nightmares, night fears; how it will all end some day, how it will all collapse; a baby touched from its first pastel perambulator by death, by the fear of eyes, of ears, of contact, the foolishness of those who do not understand, a lonely bad job of a baby — I played, and the immense bass saxophone bent over me like the frame of a somber painting. I suddenly felt, knew, that I always had and always would belong to Lothar Kinze, that I had made that entire migration of failure with him and would always be on the move with him, to the bitter end, with him and the sadness of that shabby band in the shadow of the bass saxophone as if it were a gallows, behind the girl with the broken voice like a burst bell. The faces of the German community in the audience rose, fell, intermingled. Lothar Kinze's bony fingers danced with them on two strings; individual vision, chapters, hits, tangos, and shallow foxtrots were separated by another disharmony: applause; and into it rolled the sound of the big drum from behind, to support the audience's approval with a leathery tenebrous thundering; the hunchback's glasses were raised to the spotlit forestage, and under the glasses the blue lips were released from the spasm of depression and unceasing anxiety by an almost joyful curve brought on by the distorted music that resembled him; but Horst Hermann Kühl seemed not to understand — he applauded; then a new dose of that weeping call of approximation, of imperfection: new applause; in the middle of it, a hand was placed on my shoulder; I looked at it; a white, soft hand, not a worker's hand but that of someone who earns his bread differently. The wrist disappeared into a close-fitting dazzling white cuff of a gauzy material, perhaps several layers of lace wrapped around the wrist, and above it a different, looser cuff with a black button. And a voice: "Come here. Backstage." A low voice, a loud, hoarse whisper. I looked up the length of the hand, up the arm, but the man's face (the hand was heavy, a large man's hand) was hidden behind the bend of the bass saxophone, so I got up as if I had been blinded (the applause was still sounding, the girl was bowing, the broken swan's wings flapping helplessly on either side of the tragic face), and felt the hand drag me backstage, firmly, almost roughly; it was only then that I saw him: he was a wild, hulking man, maybe forty. His hair was black, intertwined with what seemed like a leaden crown of thorns of gray hair, his eyes were wild, all black; a black mustache, a face that was almost Sicilian; he was insane, or normal at that insane moment; I recognized him; the pointed bluish chin with the crop of stubble jutted out over the white collar as it had stuck up out of the white hotel pillow earlier: it was the last stranger, the sleeping one whose place in Lothar Kinze's orchestra I had involuntarily taken; the mysterious one. "Give it here," he said roughly and almost ripped the green and purple jacket off me. Like the Swedish girl, he showed no sign of any deformation, no wound, no red flame of once-burnt flesh like the bald head of Lothar Kinze, and certainly no artificial limb or hump or hypertrophic nose, no blind eyes; he tore the alto sax out of my hand, yanked the strap over my head — the other hand was bound in a double white cuff as well; he growled; turning around, he walked out onto the stage and sat down, ramming the alto sax into the stand. Lothar Kinze's eyes caught a Kelly-green movement behind him, and as he bowed they slipped under his arm to the man's face; they were frightened; Lothar Kinze stayed bent over. The stranger (to me) reached roughly for the bass saxophone; he leaned it toward himself, he embraced it. The cut-down Caesar looked at him and grinned; the accordion player saw him too, but he only nodded; the pince-nez tumbled down the front of the gigantic nose and stayed hanging from their cord; she smiled; the man shoved the mouthpiece of the bass saxophone into his mouth, and at the same time the applause began to subside; each of the thawed, no longer quite Teutonic faces in the hall tilted toward a shoulder, and dream-filled eyes focused on the newcomer. Worriedly, nervously, Lothar Kinze squinted at the bass saxophone player, nodding slightly, questioningly; the bass saxophone player nodded too, but forcefully as if rejecting all attention. Lothar Kinze raised his bow; once again he rolled his torso in that waltz movement, he leaned his bow on the two strings and the insistent off-key introduction sounded, creeping through twelve miserable measures.

I leaned up against a backdrop; the bass saxophone player inhaled, and then a terrible, somber, prehistoric tone exploded over the stage; it jumped on the mechanical bandwagon of the waltz, drowning out everything, it absorbed the disharmony, its depths dissolved it; the man blew into the big instrument with the immense strength of frantic, desperate lungs and, as he blew, the melody of "The Bear" suddenly slowed down, crumbled, the call of the bass saxophone sounded like breathing, the player's fingers began to leap wildly along the strong, silver, matte body of the giant hookah, as if searching for something, I couldn't take my eyes off them, temporizing triplets emerged, the fingers leaped, stopped and leaped again, then grasped the body firmly; I shut my eyes; the drum and the piano sounded the mechanical three-quarter pulse beat, the orchestrionic oom-pahpah; but above it, like a dancing male gorilla, like a hairy bird of legend slowly beating its black wings, the voice of the broad metal throat screamed the bound strength of bamboo vocal chords, the tone of the bass saxophone, not in the three-quarter time but beyond it, in four heavy beats through which it slid with an immense secret yet emotive strength, in septolets, in a beat that went not only against the automatic

oom-pahpah but also against the four intended ac-
cents as if it were shaking off not only all the laws
of music but also the cramping weight of something
even more immense; a polyrhythmical phoenix,
black, ominous, tragic, rising to the red sun of that
evening from some horrible moment, from all fearful days, the Adrian Rollini of that child's dream
come true, personified, struggling — yes! I opened
my eyes: the man was struggling with the bass saxophone; he was not playing, he was overpowering
it; it sounded like the wild fight of two cruel,
dangerous, and powerful animals roaring at each
other; his ditch-digger's hands (by their size, not
their calluses) were squeezing the blinded body that
was like the neck of a brontosaurus, and huge sobs
poured out of the corpus, roars thousands of mil-
lions of years old. I closed my eyes again. But
before I submerged in the semilight of the vision,
I caught a brief shot of two rows of faces — *Lothar
Kinze und sein Unterhaltungsorchester,* and Horst
Hermann Kühl and his entourage: in its soft disso-
lution Kühl's face suddenly hardened again with
amazement; the Bavarian dream evaporated like
ether, and the softened features began quickly and
obviously to realign themselves into the long mask
of the Roman conquistador; in apposition, the spiritual semicircle of the faces in the band glowed
with an incandescent joy: the mechanism of the
waltz had undergone the squaring of the circle —

but my eyes were closed again by then, by then I saw again that flower on the illuminated stage, in the steamy sunny jungle, and the gorilla's voice of male (no, human) despair shook the stage as it did then, long ago, as it did now, as it would evermore — the swinging brasses.

It was a premature legend: Charlie Bird did not struggle with a saxophone like that, with music like that, with life like that, until later; this was a band of primordial times, obscured by the fog of another history, the war, by that island of Europe separated from the wide distant world by a narrowing ring of steel and dynamite; just as great, just as painful, but forgotten, an anonymous bass saxophone player under the canvas of a circus tent, which like the canvas-rigged *Santa Virgo Maria de los Angelos* sailed those two, three, four years over the Pacific Ocean of burned-down villages and traces of long-gone front lines; Lothar Kinze and his Side Show; it never found land, it fell apart, disintegrated in the final confusion of nations; an unknown black Schulz-Koehn, the Adrian Rollini of my dream, some great, unknown, unexplainable pain, so sad, *sehr traurig, traurig wie eine Glocke.*

Another hand touched my shoulder, I caught the flash of eyes. I turned around. Horst Hermann Kühl reached for my mustache and pulled it off. "So that's how it is," he said. "Scram!" His face was carefully aligned again into the controlled features of the mask. Dangerous, unpleasant, murderous.

I turned back. The loud mighty roar of the struggling bass saxophone still sounded from the lighted stage. "Scram!" hissed Kühl. I caught a glimpse of the stage manager, the Czech, and for an instant I awoke from the dream and the cold sweat of a chimera did chill me. But they wouldn't believe it. Not Kostelec. Not even the Kostelec inside me — later I wouldn't believe it myself, or understand it. The unattainable message of music, forever locked behind the seven locks of that talent, will always be no more than this craving to communicate, to understand, to go all the way to the end with them — the end of what? of the world, heaven, life — possibly of truth.

I fled up the iron staircase in the darkness, and then down the hotel corridor past silent doors with brass numbers, along the beige and cream hall to the door numbered 12A. The call of the bass saxophone somewhere in the distance collapsed with a sob. I opened the door and turned on the light. My jacket was hanging over a chair, my tenor saxophone part still lying on the table. I dressed in a hurry, then I stopped; there was a light on in the bathroom — I saw it through the half-open door — a light I hadn't turned on. Three steps were enough; I looked in. In the white, perhaps alabaster tub, the surface of the pink water lay motionless, quiet, like a lake in which a mermaid had bled to death; and across the white tiles and the white bathroom carpet led a trail of blood.

I stared at it, and it was an answer, though veiled, symbolical; it was after all only half an answer, but that is all we ever will get; there are no complete answers in this desperate gore of life — just a trace of blood, a trail of blood, the screaming voice of the struggling bass saxophone, so sad; only deathly pain firmly enclosed in the shell of our loneliness; he at least succeeded in giving a cry, in shaking the complacency of a dark hall somewhere in Europe; others succeed at nothing, disappearing through the anonymous trapdoors of the world, the soul, without even a whisper, without even that voice.

When I walked out of the hotel, under the stars that showed a blatant disrespect for human regulations, I could hear Lothar Kinze's sentimental music very weakly from behind the hotel, where the theater was. And in it, wrapped in a monotonous mezzoforte, an equally sentimental, equally emotionless alto saxophone.

I walked through the dark streets of the blacked-out town. No one ever found out about it (even though the stage manager recognized me, I'm certain of that) but it wasn't a dream; nor was it a hallucination, a chimera, nothing like that. True, the next day there wasn't a trace of the gray bus in town, and I had no contacts among the German community in Kostelec to confirm or deny it for me (except for Mr. Kleinenherr; I asked him, but he didn't go to Lothar Kinze's concert — he avoided the German community affairs whenever he could).

But it was no dream: for that desperate scream of youth is still inside me, the challenge of the bass saxophone. I forget it in the rush of the day, in the rush of life, and I only repeat I love you, I love you, mechanically, because the tears and the callous disinterest of the world have given me this countenance, this thick skin; but there is a memento — an intimate, truthful moment God knows where, God knows when, and because of it I shall always be on the move with Lothar Kinze's orchestra, a sad musician on the mournful routes of Europe's periphery, surrounded by storm clouds; and the somber bass saxophone player, the adrian rollini, will time and again remind me of dream, truth, incomprehensibility: the memento of the bass saxophone.

Josef Škvorecký was born in 1924 at Náchod, Bohemia, Czechoslovakia. He has worked as a laborer, a teacher, and an editor, and of his numerous writings four are available in English: the novels, *The Cowards* (1958) and *Miss Silver's Past* (1969); a book of crime stories, *The Mournful Demeanor of Lt. Boruvka* (1966); and a history of the Czech cinema, *All the Bright Young Men and Women* (1971). After the Soviet invasion of Czechoslovakia he emigrated to Canada, where he is Professor of English and Film at Erindale College in the University of Toronto. He and his wife, the writer Zdena Salivarová, live in Toronto where they run a small emigré publishing house.

A NOTE ON THE TYPE

This book was set on the Linotype in Bodoni Book, so-called
after Giambattista Bodoni (1740–1813), son of a printer of
Piedmont. After gaining experience and fame as superin-
tendent of the Press of the Propaganda in Rome, Bodoni
became in 1768 the head of the ducal printing house at
Parma, which he soon made the foremost of its kind in
Europe. His *Manuale Tipografico*, completed by his widow
in 1818, contains 279 pages of specimens of types, including
alphabets of about thirty languages. His editions of Greek,
Latin, Italian, and French classics are celebrated for their
typography. He was an innovator in type design, making his
new faces rounder, wider, and lighter, with greater openness
and delicacy, and with sharper contrast between the thick
and thin lines.

Composed by American Book–Stratford Press, Inc.,
Brattleboro, Vermont.
Printed and bound by The Haddon Craftsmen, Inc.,
Scranton, Pennsylvania.

Typography and binding design by Camilla Filancia